Graham's Resolution

Book 3

The Last Infidels

By A. R. Shaw
Liberty Lake, Washington

Publisher's Note: This is a work of fiction. Names, characters, places, and incidents are a product of the author's imagination. Locales and public names are sometimes used for atmospheric purposes. Any resemblance to actual people, living or dead, or to businesses, companies, events, institutions, or locales is completely coincidental.

Cover Design by Keri Knutson of Alchemybookcovers.com

Dedicated to my beautiful daughter,
my Sarah-Melanie
finding you . . . completed me.

Table of Contents

Welcome to the world of Graham's Resolution. As a writer, I try to limit the parts that readers tend to skip. Therefore, within these pages I do not often recount what you've already read. However, here I will attempt to inform you of what's already taken place in case my readers have forgotten between releases.

As the series begins, 80 percent of the world has died from infection with the H5N1 virus, commonly called the China Pandemic. Graham is about to bury his father, his last surviving family member, when Hyun-Ok, Bang's mother, approaches him. She dies while transferring her son to Graham and warns him of the dangers to come.

Graham and Bang then trek to the family cabin, north along the Skagit River, in the fictional town of Cascade (inspired by the town of Rockport, Washington). Along the way, they encounter a madman named Campos. Graham must kill Campos in order to keep the man from killing twin girls Macy and Marcy, who are on their way to their Dad's apartment. Sheriff, a stray police dog, also appears with the twins; he is one of the few dogs who has not yet gone to the wild side out of hunger, and he quickly becomes a loyal companion to the girls. (Sheriff has become a beloved character in the series; nearly every week I receive fan mail asking me to keep him alive.)

Together, Graham, Bang, the twins, and Sheriff make their way to Cascade, where Graham finds a grouchy old man, Ennis, and an ailing Native American woman, Tala, already occupying his cabin. The group learns to coexist until they run across a group of people dressed in hazmat suits who dump a boy named Mark into their possession.

The members of Graham's group are carriers of the virus, and the people in suits are actually members of a clever prepper organization that has anticipated all the calamities to come their way. The preppers, however, are still susceptible to the virus that Graham's group carries.

The two groups tentatively learn to live near each other, but with very specific quarantine rules. This works until one day a marauding group kidnaps Tala. The preppers aid Graham in her rescue, but one of their members, Sam, is exposed to the virus and, instead of dying, he becomes a rare carrier as well. Sadly, his seven-year-old daughter is now orphaned and has to stay with the preppers while Sam goes to live at Graham's camp. This is how book 1, *The China Pandemic*, ends—with Sam only able to visit with his young daughter at a safe distance across the Skagit River.

The winter season begins book 2, *The Cascade Preppers*. We start by learning how Sam has adjusted to the group; Graham and Tala are now in a relationship. Anything that can go wrong does in book 2: Sam takes Mark and Marcy on a hunting trip and encounters a snowstorm and disaster; Ennis becomes ill; Graham goes into town and is badly injured in a wild dog attack, but is saved by newcomer McCann, who has traveled to Cascade on horseback. There is a devastating fire at the prepper camp that causes Sam to break all quarantine rules to ensure the safety of his daughter, Addy, an effort that nearly gets him killed. The fire kills Dalton's wife Kim and several others.

At the end of book 2, the injured members of Graham's camp have recovered, but Ennis dies. Scientist Clarisse, the preppers' best asset, creates a vaccine to inoculate those who are still susceptible to the virus. These events, and the fact that Tala is now pregnant, end *The Cascade preppers* on a note of both hope and uncertainty.

With that out of the way, I now present to you *The Last Infidels*.

Dutch felt eyes upon them and could almost smell the mares' fear; the wild dogs had tracked them through the night. After the long march across the state to silently escape from the invaders, to be exposed now by dogs seemed cruel, even for fate.

He raised his hand slowly to signal the driver of the truck behind him to stop, then clenched his fist to have her cut the engine. While he held the reins a whisper's breath away from the hide of the mares pulling the wagon, Dutch slid his Remington 870 shotgun across his lap with slow stealth. In anticipation of the wild beasts, he had loaded it earlier with a combo load of two number 1 buckshot, followed by two double-ought and then two slugs, for a total of six shots. Practice taught him that loading his weapon in this way allowed extra insurance in case something just kept coming at him. If that did not work, he had other options at his disposal and within reach.

Intent on hearing even the faintest of danger signs, he leaned forward on the bench seat of the wagon and tilted his head to the best angle. Shutting his eyes in concentration furthered the conscious effort. He had ridden without care before the dark descended; the wild dogs' howling had already warned him of their carnivorous intentions come nightfall. Their glowing eyes shone through the darkening forest at regular intervals as the day lengthened into dusk.

The time to start a fire and make camp had passed, and the steady cadence of the five-ton US Army truck and trailer, loaded down with provisions, rang out as it trailed the little convoy to the outskirts of Cascade. The provisions intended for a new homestead, Dutch's mission now. He led in a wagon burdened much like the truck. Two lineback horses who were acutely aware of the present danger pulled the wagon.

The young woman driving the truck behind him had come in handy, but if it had not been for the need to drive both vehicles, Dutch would have kicked her out near the Coulee Dam on State Route 20. He was not only afraid of being tracked by the invaders but also grew worried that he was beginning to feel responsible for the safety of the woman who was a mere child in age compared to him. In his mind, the liability she posed could mean the death of both of them, and he wanted no charges now or ever again.

He planned to send her away at his earliest convenience. *She'll have to take care of herself*, Dutch kept telling the nagging voice deep within his mind. At almost fifty years of age, she appeared to be in her early twenties and needed no protector, especially not someone like him who was nearly fifty. Babysitting a whiny twenty-something—particularly in a survival situation—held not a shred of appeal to him.

Not that she was whiny, really; on the contrary, she irritated him because she did not talk. Hell, from the moment they'd met around Saint Maries, south of Coeur d'Alene, Idaho, four days earlier, she'd nearly driven him mad with her silence. Unfortunately, he had little choice but to let her tag along, since he had not run across another living soul all the way here. She was a good worker, he'd give her that. He would allow her to stick around for a few more days until she got her bearings, and he hoped that the current residents of Cascade would take her in after he warned them of the coming danger. He intended to fill a backpack for her, give her one of the mares tied to the back of the wagon for payment, and send her on her way.

The real reason he had dared take her along at all was that he knew the reality if he'd left her behind: she would have succumbed to the invaders. Since they had already entered the country, he suspected they would, by now, be hunting along Interstate 90 and taking inventory of their newly conquered land.

The invaders had simple rules, really—either join their ranks or die. They didn't bother wasting ammunition; they did the deed with brutal sincerity, using their bare hands or the blade of hatchet, knife, or sword. To kill this way was their animalistic preference. It was the same way they handled things in their own countries. Ammo they saved for hunting; slaughtering by blade was their choice for infidels and nonbelievers. They were the boots on the ground . . . only this time, it was American soil they tread upon.

China was merely the provider of the weapon, and double-crossing China wasn't difficult for them. The Chinese had the weaponized version of the virus under coolant in their labs already, so it was merely a matter of money and information to complete the exchange. What China didn't take into consideration was the need to deflect blame. Purposely exposing the Chinese for developing the virus was only fitting; it ensured that the world saw them as the only possible culprit in the death of hundreds of thousands.

Invasion was phase 3 in an elaborate five-step world domination plan for jihad. First they implemented the H5N1 virus by weaponizing it via several self-sacrificing subjects; once virulent with the deadly strain, they boarded airplanes with circulating air systems, thus making each passenger also contagious. The unsuspecting couriers then returned to their colonies to die and, in doing so, achieved genocide by spreading the virus exponentially.

Second, they waited and let the hand of death take its toll. While manipulating their own statistics to reflect a higher mortality rate than they suffered was the easiest of deceptions, the sacrifice of thousands of their own for jihad prevailed as imperative. However they committed the deed, it was essential that they use hate in any form to wipe out most of humankind—no offense was too vile, no taboo ruled out, nothing considered sacred.

Since the infiltration took place early on, Europe fell easily and was destroyed from within. Now, all that remained of the United States would soon be dominated as well. Jihad was a long-term plan. With the first steps implemented, they were gleeful with the results so far—America, as it had been, was no more.

Dutch had been on his second tour in Iraq when an improvised explosive device took out his lower left leg, right below the knee. That was it for him. Throughout his recovery and remarkable transition to prosthetic use, he had tried to convince his supervisor that he was in even better shape than before. Rules were rules, however, and section 313 of the army regulations had clearly put him in the discharge column. After a long recovery, he'd packed up his gear and headed back to the States.

After making his way to his father's abandoned ranch south of Coeur d'Alene, Idaho, he threw himself into farming and ranching with every shred of intensity he had used in war. He had no other real options. He'd never married, and his parents had passed only one year before his injury. He was happy it had happened this way; he wasn't sure if his mother could have taken it. His father, on the other hand, would have expected him to stand until the end.

His brother Clive lived in California. He'd called Dutch twice when the pandemic hit hard. The first call was to say that his wife had the virus, and the next call brought the news that their daughter had passed right after her. Dutch was not surprised to hear him say he was going to take his own life right after he hung up the phone, and he did not try to stop Clive. He couldn't blame him. What was there left to live for? He said only, "I love you, brother," before the call ended.

Dutch had heard this same sad story all over the country, and he waited to catch the inevitable virus. He welcomed its presence; he even went out to a couple of local bars—after nearly killing himself working on the ranch—in anticipation of contracting the damned thing, but it just never took hold in him. He woke up with the sniffles once and thought, *Okay, here it comes,* but in a few days they cleared up. In time he found himself, well . . . disappointed.

Dutch helped his neighbors and took care of their livestock when he could. Then they began to die off, one by one, until one day he realized he was the only one driving through town. He went around to the deceased farmers' spreads and let loose their livestock: cattle, horses, donkeys, pigs, sheep, goats, and chickens. He just opened the gates and watched them roam away, tentative at first but free to graze along with the mule deer and roaming elk herds. No one else was coming to care for them, so he figured it was his duty to let them go rather than to let them starve in their stables; at least they stood a chance at adapting to the wild side of life, rather than die outright of starvation.

Then he started listening in on radio transmissions for any traffic coming or going. He hadn't heard much until a few months ago. The first intelligent noise he heard was a Morse code transmission on the high-frequency band coming from the northeastern area of Washington state. At first he thought it was an automatic repeater beacon someone had never taken the time to turn off. Dutch was a bit rusty on translation, and it took him a while, but when he finally figured out the dits and dahs, it came as a shock to find there were more survivors out there.

He wanted to make contact, but didn't trust anyone out there just yet. He waited, leaving the option open for later. Then Dutch began overhearing transmissions of a different kind, and that set his mind reeling. He wasn't as thrilled about this new discovery. It was a voice transmission in a language he'd only run into in faraway war-torn lands where bombs lay hidden and even women and children were suspect because they, too, might kill you.

After a few days of increased activity Dutch's mind began connecting the dots. Could this whole thing have been a planned attack? There were no other inferences to make. The conspiracy theorists had been right all along. At first it had been only a suspicion that the virus was weaponized; now he was sure those suspicions were founded on truth.

Dutch rarely spoke aloud in his lone residence unless it was to his two dogs. When the reality sunk in about what the overheard transmissions meant, he said to the empty room, "You couldn't fight us man to man . . . you goddamn cowards."

After monitoring the Morse-encrypted transmissions for a few more weeks, Dutch realized that the worst of his fears had come true: an invasion of the United States was in progress. They had already sent several teams ahead to secure major cities. Hell, they were already here during the virus phase, just lying in wait and hiding in the shadows. Dutch knew they must have had some kind of vaccine available to them, or they wouldn't take the risk.

Then, after a few more weeks, the enemy moved north of him by dark of night. They were traveling the interstate highways in long, raucous convoys and clearing communities of survivors. He mounted a reconnaissance strategy to scope them out on horseback before making plans to bypass them and warn the northerners. He couldn't risk them intercepting a radio transmission from him that would expose his own location. Traveling by horseback wouldn't be too daunting; he only had to go from Saint Maries to Coeur d'Alene.

During a reconnaissance outing on a dark, cold, spring night, Dutch had heard the ramping up of hostile chatter and then witnessed the death blow as a survivor—another one who couldn't live with the intruders' ways—begged for his life; eventually the man put down his weapon and submitted to his own demise by a brutal beating not fit for even the worst of criminals.

That was the same night that Dutch had encountered the redheaded girl dressed in a black burka. She fled through the darkened forest toward him like a scared deer, nearly revealing their position; when he caught her she fought bitterly. He saw the terror and the bruising, and contemplated breaking her neck without delay to put her out of her misery; doing so would have been merciful. Instead, when she became limp in his grasp and opened her frightened light-green eyes to the horrific scene, as if trying to wake from a nightmare, he pulled her backward. Using the night to blanket their retreat, he kept her from uttering a sound until they were miles away.

When he removed his hand from her mouth, she didn't speak—not even when he asked her name. She only held onto his torso with clenched fists, gradually becoming limper as he guided her away under the cover of darkness.

Dutch didn't sleep that evening; instead, he packed up his campsite. He loaded his belongings, and then the girl—as though she were one of his possessions. Then, on horseback, they made their way back to his ranch in Saint Maries. She was asleep when they arrived at his cabin just before dawn.

He had pulled her limp, frail body down from Gus, the same lineback horse who was now in the lead of those pulling the wagon. After laying her down in the cabin, the dogs Elsa and Frank began to investigate the stranger; they nudged their wet noses into the flaming red hair that fell over her sleeping face until Dutch gave the hand signal that never failed to correct the well-trained, ex-military Belgian shepherds. Instead of investigating, they guarded her while Dutch took care of the outside chores.

Shortly after dawn the girl had opened her eyes through the sleepy veil and immediately retreated up and away from the canines until her back met the wall. She was terrified of the pair's gleaming eyes, even though their tongues lolled out of their mouths, forming ridiculous smiles for such supposedly fearsome creatures.

Dutch couldn't help himself, and he chuckled as both dogs eyed her curious behavior. As she spun in his direction, he caught her wild look —one that meant to murder him in cold blood if possible.

"Hey now," Dutch said in reproach while he signaled with one hand for the shepherds to lie down. As they moved away, so did the girl's deadly stare, and Dutch watched as her attention fought to seek which was the greater threat in her view.

"No one's going to hurt you." He paused, and then added, "Unless you try to kill me; then, forget it."

She refocused on him, not uttering a word. Then he watched as the inevitable happened: her eyes followed the line of his tall frame down the right side of his leg where instead of a boot, as expected, she saw the metal prosthesis. It never bothered him, and he'd gotten used to the occasional stares. He'd never been one to beg for sympathy, so he seldom commented on it. He wasn't angry about it either, as counselors would have had him believe. He wanted none of the bullshit that went along with being injured. To Dutch, they won if he gave them that satisfaction, so he had ignored the conclusion he knew her mind would eventually come to.

"Do your part, don't steal from me, and we'll get along fine. I'm leaving here, and I can use your help. If you don't want to go, you're welcome to stay here. I'm warning you, though: the cabin won't be safe for long with the invaders around. The decision is yours to make. You probably want time to think about it, but we don't have the luxury of time. I'm headed northwest to a camp with other people; I'll bring you with me. It'll be safer in numbers against these guys. You can come, if you help get us there. Tell me now. We leave at nightfall."

The dogs Elsa and Frank had followed the conversation and turned their heads in unison for the girl's answer. After a moment's contemplation, she simply nodded.

Dutch remembered the sullen expression she had given him that day. That was weeks ago now, and they'd finally made it into Cascade, where the Morse code message beckoned them. He'd escorted both of them safely out of danger and kept them fed. He thought she at least owed him a little faith by now, but she still didn't show any sign of trusting him—not even enough to tell him her name. And now, he figured, he'd never learn it because they were about to be eaten by ravenous wild dogs.

Of course, he wasn't about to let that happen easily; at the very least, he'd make sure they choked on every bit of him.

Macy pulled her feet out of her hiking boots and leaned back in the office chair. She propped her feet, which were covered in knitted socks, upon the metal table with loud, purposeful *thunks*. Through the pinned-back tent door, the *drip, drip* of spring rain sounded. With a heavy sigh, she turned to the next chapter of the radio manual that Rick had given her to read. She tried to engross herself into the meandering writings of someone she considered a nerdish madman.

As Macy read, the most peculiar kind of static came over the receiver. She listened for a minute, decided it was nothing more than interference of some kind, then reached over to turn the potentiometer knob down so that she could concentrate on the infuriating manual. The material was an indecipherable foreign language to her; she reread the final paragraph of the chapter three times, and still she failed to grasp Ohm's law and his definition formula for "current equals voltage divided by resistance" and "why volts matter over watts," or who would even care anymore, but Rick was relentless. She knew he wanted to keep up the standards from the old world, but this . . . this was ridiculous. "Ugh!" Macy heaved the ARRL Technician Radio manual to the floor, startling Sheriff who had just begun his afternoon nap.

"Why? Why do we need to keep up with the old rules?" she asked Sheriff, who seemed mildly disgruntled. The dog's ears perked up while he tilted his head at her question, as if to say, *Hell if I know. Don't throw things at me, woman.*

Macy's chair squeaked as she bent down and sank her fingers into his scruff, scratching him behind his ear. "You adjusted to this new life much better than the rest of us, didn't you, boy?"

She didn't think Sheriff cared much about her inquiry; he appeared to be more interested in her getting to the spot just behind and to the left of his ear. She watched as he lowered his eyelids over those deep-brown, soulful eyes as he dipped into his comfort zone.

When she was about to break the moment and retrieve the discarded manual, Rick strolled into the communications tent.

He looked at the manual on the ground, picked it up, and handed it to her. "How's it going? Any new contacts?" he asked.

As if!

"No. Same as usual. There's no one out there, Rick. It's only us. I don't even know why we try listening," Macy lamented.

He play-punched her in the shoulder. "Someday there might be. On the other hand, someday, someone else might think to listen in and find out that more people are out there. You never know, ye of little faith and hope. What's up with you today, anyway? You're usually upbeat, but I see you're somewhat down. What is it, Mace?"

She stared at him. *Darn, I'm cornered.* Rick had always annoyed Macy to no end, but he treated her in a younger sister kind of way. She didn't like that he could "see" how she felt. She'd forgotten whom she was complaining to, and now she was faced with having to "share" her feelings with him. *What could be worse?*

"Nothing, I'm fine." she lied, hoping to divert Rick from her melancholy. She avoided his gaze as she closed the manual and put on her hiking boots for the trek back to Graham's camp.

Rick scratched his bearded chin while evaluating her, and Macy could still feel his eyes on her. "Okay, if you don't want to talk about it now, that's your business. I'm here if you want to share, though. Okay?"

She blinked up at him and nodded her chin. There was a lot she was holding inside of herself. She couldn't help it. She didn't want to burden Graham—or Rick, for that matter—with her problems. Right now, her sister was far from the person she could "talk" to.

Macy often felt close to tears. The long winter was over; spring brought flowers and hope, but it rained far too much to be happy for long. Tala would understand, but she was busy dealing with fear over her unborn child, so Macy didn't want to confide in her either. As it was, they were all trying to make Tala's life easier now because she physically did too much to keep them all going. They were all trying to pave the way for a trouble-free delivery as if their future hinged on a healthy and safe birth.

Macy finished tying her boots and put on her green slicker. "Okay. Thanks, Rick," she said. She felt Sheriff bump into her calf as he ran to catch up to her in the doorway when he realized they were leaving.

In the drizzling rain outside the tent, she waved good-bye to Dalton's boys, Hunter and Kade, who were dutifully moving firewood from one location to another. The little brother stacked logs onto the bigger brother's outstretched arms. Hunter partially waved with his overburdened load and Kade called after her, "Bye, Macy!"

She smiled to herself as she set out, heading toward the crossing at Skagit River and closing the gap between this world and her own. She made the trip twice a week to take her shift at the communications tent to learn what she could from Rick . . . and to get away from Graham's camp. She did it to have a sense of normalcy and escape from something she could not name.

As she neared the rushing river she realized that, had she been with someone on her walk besides Sheriff, she wouldn't be able to keep up a conversation over the resounding roar of the water. Since spring had started and the snowpack had begun to melt, not only had the river gone from a trickle to a powerful torrent but the earth itself mixed with water and became a thick, sludgy mud. Past residents knew this time of year better as "mud season."

As the rain came down in a rapid cadence, Macy stopped a minute and zipped up her jacket so that her holstered gun would not become soaked. As Sheriff stopped, Macy noticed that the thick brown paste covered his paws.

When they hit the bridge, Sheriff hesitated until Macy was halfway across. She turned back, patted her thigh, and called to him to come to her.

"You're really a big sissy, aren't you?" she asked him as he scampered across, ran ahead of her, and continued to the other side of the river. Once she had traversed the wooden planks, her boots sank into the moist earth, and it took effort not to slide in the slick, messy mire before she gained footing on the rockier ground.

They headed into the forest, where the raindrops had a harder time reaching them through the evergreen canopy. Instead of her feet sinking into the mud, they fell on a bedding of soft needles that emitted a fresh pine aroma with each step. This section was the part of the trip Macy liked the best. She felt more at peace hidden within the forest, almost as if she were in her own mind entirely and left to figure out her worries in silent contemplation. As she often did, she lingered under the veil on her path home as she sifted and sorted through all the confusing events of both past and present. Here was where she had spent most of her time in the days following Ennis's death because she felt him here the most. Graham had found her here in the woods on more than one occasion. He knew she needed her space, and had only asked that she let him know before she left the camp.

Macy respected Graham's request and didn't stay out too long because she didn't want him to be concerned about her. And even though her pace slowed, she too soon came to the light that broke at the end of her journey. Macy and Sheriff emerged just as the rain subsided and the crack of a hammer drove a nail home.

Sheriff ran ahead to greet Bang as they entered the clearing at Graham's camp. Bang stood near the ladder, waiting patiently to hand Graham the next cedar shake, ready for its place among the others on the roof of the new partition. Graham held a nail between his lips and mouthed, "Hello" to Macy when he saw her.

He watched as she beamed a smile in return, but her posture wasn't in it. Graham was worried about both her and Bang; both of them had withdrawn from the group since Ennis's death. He suspected Bang was mourning Ennis, but also torturing himself about his role in Addy's disability—the boy had been the one to expose her to the virus that left her deaf. With Macy, he figured Ennis's death just exacerbated her grief over her own parents' deaths and the uncertainty of life in general.

There was nothing Graham could do to change it; optimism was in short supply these days. He finished the nail with one more whack and then pulled the next one out of his mouth quickly so he could speak unhindered. As she headed for the cabin door, he called out, "Hey, Macy?"

She stopped in her tracks and turned to look at him. "Yeah?"

He couldn't think of the words to say. He wanted to fix her, to mend her. He wanted to say, "You are going to be fine," but he could only stare at her standing there with muddy boots, a frown, and Sheriff by her side.

"What, Graham?"

"Uh, could you take the clothes off the line for Tala? They aren't going to dry in this rain. We're going over to Clarisse's for a visit." *Yeah, that's good. Some work will make her feel better.* Isn't that what his mother always used to say? Something about idle hands being a bad thing . . . too much time to think.

"Sure, just a sec," Macy said; she continued on her moping journey up the porch to retrieve the basket.

Graham then looked down at Bang and realized he'd been out there with him all morning working, and he was nothing more than a sad sack. Every attempt to brighten the boy only brought him down further. Everything he tried was wrong; nothing seemed to work. *It's all bullshit*, Graham thought.

Suddenly the opposite of what his mother had taught him popped into his mind. He remembered his mother saying, "Grim was catching" and to "Grim-up" when he and his sister were cutting-up in public—which of course only brought them into another fit of giggles. Now, the older he got, the more he thought his mother had been a master of reverse psychology.

What the hell was that about?

Dalton was having the same problem over at the preppers' camp. He was not only dealing with the loss of his wife but also coping with two grief-stricken young sons. In fact, the entire camp was still getting over the loss of four members. The weight of it all made his longtime friend somewhat, but understandably, distant and angry at times.

Graham pounded the next nail into position with more force than was necessary and reached down to retrieve the shingle offered from Bang. He tried a smile on the boy, not expecting it to work. "You want to go with Tala and me later to see Clarisse? Maybe Addy will be around. You can see for yourself that she's fine."

Bang shook his head and even looked hurt at the suggestion.

Dammit, Graham thought. *That's it. I won't even try anymore. They'll just have to come around in their own time.*

"Okay. All done," Graham said as he hammered the last nail in the plank that finished off the roof to the new partition. He climbed down the ladder and pulled it away. "Go let Tala know we're leaving for the prepper camp after I get cleaned up."

Without a word, Bang shot off inside while Graham looked on in frustration. He collapsed the ladder and headed for the new shop to put it away. At least they'd managed to get both buildings updated before the hot summer arrived. Having McCann and Mark around made work go much faster. Though they lived for the most part without electricity, they opted to use a generator for the power tools, and that enabled them to get things done much faster.

It weighed on Graham, how these kids were going to grow up with aging gasoline and how they were going to live in the future. He and Dalton were having some serious talks about the younger generations and how the adults might be able to set them up now to live. They'd either have to teach them how to live without life's conveniences like power, modern medicine, and processed goods, or they would perish. It was a harsh task, with tremendous consequences if they failed. Graham couldn't get over feeling as if humanity had already been defeated by being dependent on one way of doing things, and this was an opportunity to begin again. *Still*, he thought, *it's too soon to worry about this.* They had not recovered enough yet from humanity's last catastrophe.

Graham pulled off his soiled shirt, and even though it was still cool with the spring breeze, he bent over and used the hose to shower the sweat off his torso, face, and neck. When he looked up, he saw Tala walking toward him. Her beauty mesmerized and startled him beyond the cold shock of the icy water; at six months pregnant, she not only glowed with motherhood but was more beautiful than any woman he'd ever known. Graham could tell she appreciated his observations by the smile she beamed back at him.

"Will you stop?" she said. "Come on, or we'll be walking back in the dark!"

"We could drive, you know."

"It's good for me to walk. It's not that far."

He grabbed a damp shirt off the clothesline, put it on, and began buttoning it up. "Isn't this funny? It's like we're going to the doctor for a prenatal checkup."

"Yeah; I was always in favor of natural birth, but I never thought I'd be doing it without the option of hospitals at all."

"Well, at least we have Clarisse and Steven if anything goes wrong. They're better than nothing," Graham said as he finished buttoning his shirt and laced his rifle over his shoulder. He grabbed his cane, took Tala's hand in his, and then headed for the trail to the prepper camp—at a slower pace these days, since his wild dog attack.

"That's what I was just thinking about actually. What is Bang's generation going to do when they're our age?"

"What do you mean?" she asked.

"They won't have the benefit of Clarisse or Steven for medical care, Dalton and me for leadership, or your food preserving and gardening skills."

"Well, I thought that's what we were all doing—teaching them what we know and how to go forward. Clarisse is teaching Addy all she knows about medicine. Hunter and Kade are in training for leadership and defense. Bang is going to be a master huntsman; no one will ever go hungry with him around. McCann says Bang can also name any plant he points to already, and the little guy helps me gather herbs and natural plants for foraging with what's available in the spring without making deadly mistakes. I think it will all happen naturally; each child will find what he or she enjoys most and seems to have a knack for. You worry too much," she kidded him.

"Ha! I don't think I can worry enough. In fact, I'm sure I'm forgetting something vital; I just don't know what it is yet," he said.

Their conversation had to stop as Graham guided Tala over the loud and furious river. The pause gave him a chance to think about what she had said; he knew she was mostly correct, but he couldn't help thinking they were missing something. They didn't have enough people between the two camps to learn and develop a new society that would last and grow. As they walked past the bridge, the noise lessened, and he continued their conversation.

"Right now, we're working from sunup to sundown, and we'll need to do that until it starts snowing again. Then we'll use the winter downtime to repair our equipment, tan hides, and make up anything we forgot or didn't have time for in the warmer months. Our child," he said, placing his hand on Tala's stomach, "will depend on the younger generation getting it right the first time. There's no room for costly mistakes."

"I know," Tala said, trying to ease his concerns. "But at least we have the preppers now, too. Macy's been there learning how to operate the radio, McCann is there right now, helping Sam tan hides, and we're working on getting cows together. This"—she raised her arms to gesture to their new environment—"is like a little town now. It's a new beginning. We're starting to *thrive* now, not just survive. It will all work out, Graham."

"It's hell in the winter. We've got two depressed kids on our hands, and I'm terrified you're going to name the baby after Ennis."

Tala laughed. "Well, there is that . . . Don't you see, Graham? We've made it. Yes, we lost Ennis, but we've gained Addy. Yes, the kids are still mourning, but don't you think they deserve enough time to get over their grief? They have to go through the pain to recognize happiness. They'll get better in time. Let them grieve as much as they need to," she said as she ran one hand over the nape of his neck. "You're still grieving too, I can see it," she said in a soothing tone and leaned into him as they walked together. "By summer they'll be fine and we'll have a new one with us. And life will go on."

Graham kissed her on the temple as they made their way down the trail sprinkled with spring's wildflowers. Soon, through the trees, the quarantine building could be detected, if you knew where to look. They greeted the sentry guard as they entered the doorway. "What, no pat-down this time? You guys are getting lax."

The guard chuckled at Graham. "She's down in her office, as usual."

"Thank you." Tala grinned at him.

When they came to the doorway, they could see Clarisse was deep in thought as she peered down her microscope, and her "mini-me," Addy, wasn't far away, reading a rather large book for a girl her age and totally engrossed in the subject in front of her.

Graham knocked on the doorframe. "Hello, Doctor . . . hey, what is your last name, anyway?"

Clarisse looked up and, deflecting the question, said, "You can just call me Clarisse. I'm happy to see you guys today." When she stood, the motion caused Addy to lift her head, and the girl's bright smile showed she was happy to see them too. She walked over and gave Graham and Tala a hug.

Tala signed, *Hello. What are you reading?*

Addy raised her small hands and nimbly signed *book* then looked perplexed. She stepped back and glanced at Clarisse for clarification on how to sign what she wanted to say and then spelled out *on human anatomy.*

Graham marveled at the girl; she'd been through so much and yet had tremendous resilience. Two months ago, the dreaded virus that had taken so many had nearly claimed Addy, but Clarisse fought back and pulled the girl from death's door, though she couldn't say for certain that the virus wouldn't ever manifest itself in illness again. Now nearly eight years old, Addy was already showing a great aptitude for learning beyond her age range; her disability wasn't dampening the girl's free spirit one bit.

Even her father, Sam, admonished anyone who tried to coddle Addy. If anything, he encouraged her to learn to cope; he took her deep into the woods daily and taught her how to feel the vibrations of her surroundings. The slight picking up of a breeze through the trees meant someone or something had passed her nearby. To feel a tremor through her soles near the Skagit meant the river ran higher with the melting snow than the day before.

Graham knew Sam was trying to anticipate his daughter's life without the sense of sound and how to prepare her for coming challenges. Graham had never seen such dedication from a father and hoped to emulate the man with his own children.

"So you're here for a prenatal checkup? How funny is that?" Graham heard Clarisse say to Tala.

"Yes," Tala said. "The baby has been kicking a lot lately."

"That's good news," Clarisse said, leading them into an examination room adjacent to her office.

Graham helped Tala get onto the table Clarisse had readied for her, then helped her lean back.

"We'll listen to the heartbeat first with this special Doppler stethoscope. It allows me to hear the baby's heartbeat better than a regular stethoscope," Clarisse explained as she adjusted the sensor over the ultrasound gel she'd applied to Tala's belly. Right away, a *whooshing* sound emitted through the device in Clarisse's hand. She angled the sensor around until a strong thrumming began. Graham smiled; he couldn't help himself. His gaze met Tala's, and he thought, *This moment may be the happiest we've had since it all began.*

Graham then remembered doing this with his first wife, and pushed the memory away as fast as he could. *Not now.* But along with the memories came the hurt and an odd feeling of betrayal—even though, given the circumstances, he knew Nelly would understand.

He turned his head and saw Addy leaning in the doorway; Clarisse saw her, too. "Do you guys mind if she listens in? I mean, *participates*," she said, quickly catching herself and winking at Tala. "She's my official understudy."

"Of course not," Tala said, and Clarisse motioned for Addy to join them.

Clarisse placed the Doppler stethoscope unit in Addy's hands and signed to her to close her eyes and focus on the vibrations coming through the speaker. Graham was confused by this gesture, but as Addy's expression changed from contemplative to a bright smile, he got it. She could still feel the heartbeat vibrating through the Doppler unit she held in her hands.

"So she can feel the vibrations, huh?" Graham commented. In addition to the expectation of hearing his own child's heartbeat, he was in awe of an experience that he'd thought would be completely lost to Addy. She could *feel* the baby's heartbeat!

Addy's grin was contagious, and Graham noticed Tala discretely wiping her own happy tears away. Addy signed *fast and strong* to Tala, then handed the unit back to Clarisse and placed her hand on Tala's belly, hoping for the same vibration.

Clarisse spoke to them as Addy continued to feel for vibrations.

"The baby's heartbeat sounds perfect for this stage in your pregnancy. Any pains or minor contractions?"

"No, none at all."

"Good; I'd like to take a blood sample and run some tests. Keep taking the prenatal vitamins and only do what you feel is safe. No strenuous movement."

Graham was thinking it, and didn't want to ask, but had to. "Any chance we can tell if the baby will have the virus from the blood tests?"

"I'm afraid not. We'll have to wait and see. There's something else I should tell you," she said and took a deep breath in anticipation of their reaction.

Graham didn't like the sound of that. "What? What is it?"

"I've never actually delivered a baby before."

Graham's eyes became round orbs and Clarisse put one hand on his knee to still his reaction.

"I've done my share of surgeries. I've seen it done. I'm versed in all the complications and I'm confident I can do it, but I've never actually done it."

"Okay, now I'm nervous as hell." Graham didn't mind saying so as his own heartbeat increased rapidly.

Tala tried to reassure him. "I'm sure she'll do fine, Graham."

Addy had covered Tala's belly after wiping off the gel, and Graham watched as Tala signed to the child, *You are going to make a wonderful doctor.*

He had to agree.

Thank you, Addy returned, then scampered off to resume her reading.

Graham asked Clarisse, "Did she have a hard time at all with the hearing loss?"

"Oh, yeah; Sam and I spent nearly three days with a devastated little girl. Neither one of us slept. We were with her around the clock. Then on the fourth day, she just seemed to put the anguish behind her. I began teaching her sign language, and Sam is teaching her how to live using her other senses, as you know. It hasn't been that long, and she has adjusted remarkably well. She seems to have made the choice to simply put it behind her."

"That's amazing," Graham said.

"How's Bang doing?" Clarissa asked. "The last time we talked, he was still having a hard time coping."

"He still is. I keep asking him if he'd like to come and see Addy for himself, that she's fine. He won't, though. He's still dealing with that and with Ennis's death. It's been hard on Macy, too."

"Well, give them time," Clarisse suggested.

"We will. They both have to grow up too fast in this world," Tala said.

"How are Dalton's boys doing?" Graham asked.

"They're both very different kids, and each is dealing with it in his own way." She shook her head and closed her eyes. "It's awful that these children have witnessed so much. Let's hope those days are behind us and we can start moving forward again."

Graham could not agree more; perhaps having this new life within Tala would bring back their confidence. Where there had been so much death, the prospect of a birth brought hope to all of them.

Over the nervous whinny of his horses, the snap of a distant twig followed by an ominous growl brought Dutch's eyes open in an instant. In calculating the rapid advance, he only had time to rise from the wagon's bench seat. At the same time, he lifted the long shotgun by the pistol grip and aimed just ahead of where his target would be in a nanosecond. Without the proper hold, the first resounding shot rang through his entire body and sent shock waves through the air. The recoil sent the weapon straight up, but he got a hold of it on its way down.

Dutch quickly chambered the next round and fired again; the shot caught the second of what looked to be a pack of six wild dogs. The first rounds were buckshot, designed to take down their targets with a spray. That took care of the first few, but the rest continued to advance.

He had anticipated a pack and had loaded the gun with a triple-combo load. The next rounds were double-ought buckshot, a larger pellet size than the number 1 buckshot, which took down the third and fourth dogs. They kept coming, though, and the fifth one was going for the mare's belly, causing the wagon to sway when she jerked away. Dutch pumped and chambered again, saying "Steady" to the mare before he fired the last set of his shotgun's load. The lead slugs, meant as a coup de grace, stopped the attacking dog in its tracks. With his ears still ringing, he quickly pumped again as the sixth dog came right for him. With no more than three feet of space between them, he aimed straight at the furry beast's face and fired as it sprung from its haunches, aiming for Dutch's chest, fangs barred.

Aware of a piercing scream coming from the truck behind him, he pulled his pistol out of his holster and his knife from its sheath and stood ready for whatever came at him next.

He turned to see the girl leaning out of the truck window and screaming while Elsa and Frank barked their heads off in the cab. He sheathed the knife again and held up one hand, fisting it for the dogs to see. They cut their barking, but the girl still screamed relentlessly.

"Hey, knock it off all right? Do you want more to come?" he yelled in frustration. He then added, "I'm running out of ammo here, for crying out loud." He shook his head skyward and muttered, "*Now she chooses to talk,*"

"I didn't . . . I . . . I didn't know what to do," she said.

Dutch rolled his eyes, but he knew she was scared out of her wits. They'd been on the road too long, and he probably would be scared too if he'd had watched the entire grizzly scene. He took a deep breath and kicked off the dead weight of the wild dog that had landed partway on the wagon. As he climbed down, he stepped over the pile of would-be assassins. At least they were beasts and not human, but at any rate, the danger and lessons were the same: be vigilant or die.

"It's all right, Miss. You did the right thing by keeping the dogs inside the cab and keeping yourself safe." As he looked up at the young lady, he was reminded why, on some level, he appreciated her: even though she was terrified, she had done what he'd told her to do. *No matter what happens, stay in the goddamn cab. Let me handle things. You'll only get in my way and get us both killed if you act.*

Perhaps she'd seen too much in her recent past. Perhaps she was a quick learner and was adjusting to this new way of life, like the rest of them. Whatever the case might be, it was a sign that she was beginning to trust him. He had known many men in war with less aptitude to keep their heads and do as they were told. Had she let Elsa and Frank go, he would surely have lost at least one of them. Had she left the cab, the wild dogs would have gone for her, and he would have lost his advantage.

Dutch looked around into the darkness once again and decided it was as good a time as any to make camp; they could explore more in the morning. If anyone had heard the shots, they would find Dutch and the girl soon, and that was his plan. He figured the people he had heard on the radio had to be ex-military, and they'd scout out the source of the gunfire if they heard it. If his hunch was correct, it was best to make it clear he was no danger to them. Camping for the night in the open and then exploring in the morning was their best option.

"Let's go ahead and make camp here tonight," Dutch said; he opened the cab door and signaled the dogs to come out of the truck. They both made a beeline to sniff out the offenders. Dutch held his hand out to help the young woman step down, but she refused his offer and he turned away frustrated again. Then he thought better of it and decided to get it off his chest. "I'm not trying to seduce you or anything, you know. You do understand that, right? I'm old enough to be your father."

"I know," she yelled at his abrupt openness. "I'm not saying you are. But I don't want you to think I'm weak; I can do things for myself."

"Hey, I get that, but you could at least trust me enough to handle your name. Calling you *lady* is getting a little old, and I need to be able to get your attention quick if there's a problem. At least trust me that much."

She nodded her head and looked over at the carnage as the two Belgian shepherds sniffed out the beasts. She was terrified most of the time, and watching the wild dogs attack Dutch reminded her how impossible it was for a person to survive alone in this world. It took more strength than she contained within herself.

She didn't want to need anyone, but she knew she needed Dutch. Seeing the attack and hearing the savagery before the blasts shed further light on how easily she could be left to survive on her own once again. It brought her back to the violence she'd barely escaped by another beast before she'd run into Dutch that fateful night four days ago. She didn't want it to happen again. She'd killed the man, but not before he nearly killed her.

She'd been lucky enough to get to his gun, shoot him, and run like hell, still bearing the splatter of his blood upon her skin. Because of this, trust in any man would never come to her easily again. She knew Dutch was as good a guy as they came in life, but she'd never give another man her true name again; a fake one might suffice for now. A strong name . . . not a sissy-girl name.

"Liza," she said to him.

Her green-flecked eyes shot at him, and he knew right away. "You're lyin', but that'll do enough for now. Let's make camp," he said and left her standing shocked while he checked the horses.

That evening, Rick checked the video feeds once again and called Macy at Graham's camp. "Faint shots fired. What's up, kid? You guys have some furry fangs your way? Over."

"That did not come from us, Rick. Over," Macy confirmed with a hint of fear and dread in her voice.

Dalton stood next to Rick, overhearing the conversation as he buckled the holster around his middle. Rick watched Dalton as he checked his magazine and ensured there was one extra in the chamber before holstering the weapon.

"The shots were pretty far away, Dalton. Do you really think you need to go out there now?"

"They were close enough to check out. I'll take Steven. Tell Graham to stand ready."

Rick keyed the microphone. "Have Graham stand ready. Over."

"Too late, our team is already on recon. Over," Macy said.

"Hey, you guys are supposed to consult with us before you act. Over," Rick said.

"Says who? You're not the boss of us here. Besides, I was just calling you when you beeped me. Over."

Rick shook his head. "It's not *beeped*, Macy. It's *called*. Over."

"Oh, forgive me for forgetting your radio protocol," Macy said sarcastically.

"When I get a hold of you, kid . . ."

"You'll have to catch me first. And you forgot *over*. Over."

"Out!" Rick yelled.

"That kid!" Rick swore to Dalton, who only chuckled.

"She outwitted you, Rick. You've finally met your match. Get used to it." Dalton zipped up his jacket, donned his camo knit hat, and grabbed and checked the radio Rick handed to him.

"Key in three clicks for *all is clear*."

"Gotcha."

Just as Dalton turned for the door, Steven arrived geared up. "Ready?" Steven asked.

Both men hustled out of camp into the dark cover to investigate the shots fired nearby. These little missions worried Rick the most; with all the dangerous assignments they'd headed out to in the past, it was the little, unexpected ones that took out your buddy. Something like this—unexpected and quick—made wives into widows and children into orphans. They knew the ever-present danger more than anyone there did, but the reality was that the risk couldn't be helped. Rick reminded himself that Dalton was already a widower and his boys were without a mother. Steven was just Steven in Rick's mind . . . more like a brother and uncle to his own family. Steven was a permanent fixture, and Rick couldn't imagine life without him.

Rick rechecked the monitors and scanned for radio signals through the local channels. Before long, Dalton keyed in three times by using the microphone receiver's PUSH TO TALK button, the PTT, to let Rick know that all was clear. Rick expected the noise to repeat every few minutes until they returned. The method allowed Dalton to relay information back to Rick without speaking their position aloud to anyone who might overhear them.

Rick leaned back in his chair, listening to the rhythmic sounds of static from the receiver as it went through the automatic scanning procedure. He drummed his fingers on his balding head, thinking of how far they'd come and trying to anticipate the dangers awaiting them in the future.

So far he'd taken on Macy to mentor for technology. She showed the most interest and aptitude, even though she seemed reluctant to enjoy her position these days. He expected the loss of

Ennis to be difficult for her, though she'd get over his death in time. She was a tough girl with a deep heart, and he could see she meant to guard it. Being set up for pain by caring too much for others was something he could see she tried to control. At first he was a little worried, in a fatherly type of way, that McCann might try to have a relationship with the girl too soon. But she had flat-out rejected him after Ennis passed. He knew the young man cared for her, but he was going to have to bide his time before Macy was ready for any kind of romance. She wasn't like her sister, Marcy, at all. For twins, they couldn't be more different in personality.

With such a limited postpandemic society, pairing up the young seemed to be something the older adults had on their minds lately. His wife openly wondered who would be the best mate for their daughter Bethany. She was way too young still—at least nine years away from even thinking seriously about boys. In the old world, Rick would never in a million years have wanted to start considering who would marry his daughter. The suitors were everywhere, but now, in this life, with an extreme lack of inventory of young males, matchmaking had come to be something of a pastime to wager on. *None of them is good enough for Bethany.* Rick's thoughts were interrupted when he heard the scanner suddenly catch on a station broadcasting faint dits and dahs.

"What the hell?" He jumped forward in his chair and hand-tuned the potentiometer knob up for better signal strength while he grabbed a pen and a pad of paper to decipher what he identified immediately as Morse code. His hands started shaking, and a rising sense of dread filled him the farther he got into the message.

-.-. .-.. --. / .-. .. -.-. -.- / . -- .-. --. / -.- .. .-.. .-.. / ... .. --. / ....- -.. .... ..- -. . - . .-. .... / . - / ..- .-. / -.... / .---- ..... .---- / -.- .-. .-.. .. -.-. -.- ... / -.. . / -.. ..- - -.-. .... / .. .. / -.- .. .-.. .-.. / ... .. --. / -.-. ..- .-.. / ---.. ---..

CLG RICK EMRG KILL SIG HEADHUNTERS AT UR 6 151
KLICKS DE DUTCH II KILL SIG CUL 88

"Holy hell," Rick said after he laboriously deciphered the signal. Before it repeated, he grabbed for the local microphone. He hit the PTT once. He couldn't risk transmitting and exposing the team's position, but if it didn't work, he'd have no choice. They might be walking into their own deaths. The implications of the message churned in his mind.

Headhunters here? Goddamn them!

He bypassed the click warning and pressed the PTT button again. "Dalton, stop. Abort mission. I repeat, abort mission. Return to base. Do you copy? Over."

"Copy, Rick. Return to base. Out." Dalton answered with a bit of confusion in his voice, but thankfully he sounded compliant.

Rick began to put down the radio and then thought of Graham walking into a possible trap. "Shit," he said and called in to Macy.

"Twin two, over?"

He knew he sounded hurried but this was an emergency. Who knew where Graham and his team were at this point? Soon he heard Macy pick up with, "Twin two here, over."

"Call Graham, Macy. Have him return to base. Then stay off the radio completely. Don't let anyone use them, even the walkies. Over."

"Why, what's going on? Over."

"Just do it, Mace. It's urgent. No questions. Out."

As soon as he cut off the signal, he reached for the kill switch to the automatic transmitter beacon that he used to broadcast the "welcome survivors" message. He'd set it up to repeat the same phrase every hour of the day, every day. Now that he thought about it, it made him sick to know he might be responsible for leading attackers to his own people. Next he checked the wall map for what 151 klicks south of their position might be.

"Seattle," he said, dragging his finger on the map. He waited while the Morse code warning started its repeat. The melodic dits and dahs rang out and sent Rick into a worried trance until he heard Dalton and Steven's heavy footsteps in the doorway.

"What the hell, Rick? What happened?" Dalton asked.

"Listen."

"Yeah?" Steven asked.

"It's Morse. It's a warning for us. It's coming from a local station," Rick explained.

"What's the warning?" Dalton asked.

Rick read from his notes again, deciphering the military terms into layman's terms as he went. Calling Rick. Emergency. Kill signal. Headhunters south of your location, 152 kilometers. This is Dutch. I repeat. Kill signal. See you later. Love and kisses."

Nothing but silence ensued as the other two men digested the news.

"Where . . ." Steven began to ask.

"Seattle."

"The shots earlier?"

"Dunno."

"You call Graham?" Dalton asked.

"Yeah. He should be back by now, I would think."

Dalton's concerned expression turned to confusion and now looked nothing less than ominous.

Steven cleared his throat, and Rick knew that he too could feel the waves of hate emanating from Dalton. "Do you think it's a trick?"

After an uncomfortable silence, Dalton said, "It damn well better be. The shots earlier might be from this guy, Dutch, letting us know he's in the area. Though, I've never known anyone to shoot like that as a warning."

"He knows Morse. Probably former military," Rick said.

"What scares the shit out of me is what this guy is warning us about. *Headhunters.* If it's true, that can only mean one thing, Steven said, remembering the term slapped onto the extreme jihadists after their favored barbaric execution style. After al-Qaeda became meek in the shadow of the Islamic Nation, they'd been nicknamed the Headhunters. The common term among the military meant they were nothing more than unredeemable savages.

"Yeah—that terrorists have invaded us." Dalton finished for him and then exploded. "How the fuck are they even still alive?"

Rick jumped, then saw that he wasn't alone; Steven also stepped back. To piss off Dalton was to bring about the bad side of God, and no one wanted to see that.

Dalton stood with his hands on his hips, breathing fumes as the implications of the warning took hold.

"You turned off that damn beacon?" Dalton shot off at Rick.

"Yeah; right away," Rick confirmed and took a deep breath as his heart pounded within his chest. "So, you think this guy is right, and the terrorist Headhunters are south of us in Seattle? Which means, they've crawled out from the slime-covered rocks they hid beneath and have come here?"

"Rick, you idiot; it means the virus *was* weaponized . . . by *them*," Dalton said. He stood back and tried to stem his anger by lacing his hands behind his head as he looked toward the tent ceiling. "We've been so naive. It means they must have had a vaccine all along and they just committed vast genocide . . . the worst ever perpetrated by man. And now they're here to finish the job."

"What the hell do we do?" Steven said.

"We wait. Stay off the damn airwaves and wait until we hear from this Dutch guy," Dalton said.

Rick nodded. Then something occurred to him. "The message came on the HF band. He's close by, within fifteen miles. So he must have been farther away when he heard my beacon message. That means he came here to set up this warning. He came within range because he didn't want them to hear him if they were monitoring the waves. That's the only thing that makes sense. I used the Near Vertical Incident Skywave antenna to send the low-powered Morse code over the eighty-meter band on a repeat. It's not easily traceable."

"How did he know our location?" Dalton asked.

Rick looked sheepish. "Because our beacon transmission contained our coordinates and I signed it 'Rick'," he replied.

"Okay, make sure everything is turned off for now. My guess is this guy is our shooter, and we'll hear from him soon. Let's put everyone on high alert. He might be a scout for the Headhunters. We can't trust him until we know more."

"How are we going to warn Graham if we can't use the radios?" Steven said.

Dalton checked his watch. "It's late. They already know to stay off the waves. I think we're safe for tonight. I'll ride over in the morning."

"Should we tell the others?" Steven said.

"No, not yet; this could be a hoax. I have a feeling it's not, but let's not go there yet. We may have to send a scout team to make sure what this guy says is true. We'll talk with Graham tomorrow and try to make contact with the guy. Keep watch on the monitors. I'll relieve you at two."

Rick acknowledged the order and waved at his two comrades as they vacated the media tent before turning back to his equipment. He began to check everything and set to work making sure there were no other residual signals broadcast over the waves. He kept all the monitoring equipment on and even made notes to enhance views where dark shadows lay in the night.

Graham remained still as he sat astride the horse that McCann found wandering loose through town one day and had trained especially for him. The mount had become his steady land legs since his injury, which had left him with a limp. McCann had called the beast Rocket, but Graham soon changed it to Mosey to match his own speed. The horse was especially beneficial this evening since he and the boys — Mark and McCann — spotted a lone campfire at a distance through the forest.

"What do you want to do?" McCann whispered.

Graham looked around through the night. "I think we should at least check it out at a safe distance and find out how many there are."

McCann agreed, and Mark turned his horse in that direction.

"Wait, Mark. I think you should stay here and keep watch."

Mark's shoulders visibly sunk an inch, but he obeyed Graham's command. McCann picked up on the disappointment.

"We'll be right back. Hoot if you see anyone else, okay?"

Graham was impressed with McCann's diplomacy. He knew it was likely that Mark would become jealous of McCann's new foreman role in the group, especially since McCann was only a little older. What surprised Graham was that McCann also had the ability to recognize how his own dynamic in the group could alter Mark's position and cause conflict, something they all wished to avoid.

Instead, McCann took Mark on as equal and deferred decisions to him often to show him he wasn't a threat; for good measure, he never laid eyes on Marcy either. Her indignant nature didn't interest him, anyway, so that wasn't a problem.

Everyone but Macy knew she was the girl for him. McCann would wait for her to grow up. She was only sixteen, and he twenty — not a great gap in age at world's end. Graham had pointed out her young age only once, but he hadn't needed to; McCann had her honor in regard, and Graham knew he could trust him with her.

Graham noticed that Macy rejected even sitting next to McCann at the kitchen table, however. He kept his eye on the situation from afar. As much as he'd come to love Mark, he also enjoyed having McCann there at the camp; if McCann and Macy found their way to one another, that would be fine. She meant the world to everyone. She was a tough girl with a heart of gold, and Graham was thankful that McCann could see that and seemed to be biding his time.

As Graham and McCann ambled through the dark thicket of pines, the glow of the distant fire grew brighter. Graham raised his leather-gloved hand to stop their movement. Inching any closer would only alert the stranger he'd seen bending over the fire with a branch to adjust the logs. Highlighted by the fire's glow was a young woman sitting on his opposite side. She looked to be no more than twenty or so and was taking stringy bites off a chunk of jerky. McCann sucked in his breath when he saw her toss a bit of the meat. They hadn't noticed the two dogs, camouflaged by a fur blanket wrapped around the woman.

The fire stirrer moved, and when he did Graham caught a reflective glow off his previously obscured lower limb. Where his leg should have been, there was a prosthesis, but it didn't seem to hinder the man in the least.

Graham worried about the dogs detecting their position if they stayed any longer, so he motioned to McCann to back up. He took one last look at the newcomers' camp and all seemed well. Having rifles within reach, a loaded wagon, and an army truck was relatively normal these days. In fact, he'd have been surprised if they were *not* that geared up.

After they had returned to Mark, Graham spoke a hair above a whisper to both young men. "They're probably passing through. He may have had problems with wolves or wild dogs earlier when we heard the shots. We'll let Dalton's group know in the morning, and see what's up with them. At least we know the location; we can come back in the morning and see if they've left."

"Shouldn't we keep watch?" McCann said.

"No. I don't see any trouble with these two unless we startle them. I say we let them mind their own business. They don't know we're here, and they don't need any help, by the looks of things. They're well provisioned, and the girl seems to be there of her own free will."

McCann nodded in agreement and they headed back to camp.

~ ~ ~

"We have to stay off the radios," Macy said as Graham and the others walked through the door.

"Why?" he said, taking off his muddy boots and jacket.

"Rick said to. I'm not sure why. He sounded pretty serious. No one is to use the radios at all; not even the walkies."

"Okay. I'm sure they have their reasons. We'll wait and see what's up."

"We found a camp, though," Mark relayed. "Maybe they know the radio frequency we use and they're monitoring everything we say. I'll bet that's why Rick wants us to stay off the waves."

"They didn't appear to be dangerous, but yeah, we should stay off the air, then. We don't know who they are yet," McCann said.

Graham moved his stiff leg, trying to stretch out some of the tight muscles that the cold had caused. Tala approached, and she wasn't smiling; worry lines creased the bridge of her nose between her eyes. Graham embraced her and said, "I'm sure it's nothing; just

49

a precaution. Dalton will probably be here at first light. We saw the newcomers at a distance. It appears to be a man and a woman with two dogs and a few horses. They seemed well provisioned; I don't think they're trouble."

"Did they see you?" Tala asked.

"No. I don't think so," Graham said.

"Good. Come and have dinner—all of you," she said, leading the way.

The table was set, and they could smell the aroma of fresh bread. What Graham thought might be navy bean soup sat alongside a fresh salad of spring greens. They couldn't get enough greens after having to endure nothing but canned vegetables for far too long.

With everyone seated, McCann asked, "Where's Sheriff?"

"He's watching the chickens," Bang answered.

"Uh . . . you're sure that's a good idea?" Graham asked.

"He seems to like them. He doesn't try to go after them. He thinks they're pets, too."

"Okay. Let's make sure we let him out after dinner then," Graham said as more than one suppressed chuckle came from around the table. He didn't want to dash Bang's authority, but he was certain that if Sheriff got hungry enough, he'd eat one of their new feathery pets pretty quickly.

"This is great soup, Tala," Graham said, appreciating how it chased the damp chill away from him.

"Don't thank me. McCann started the beans this morning and then Macy finished it this evening," Tala informed him.

Graham looked down the table at McCann. "Man of many talents, I see," he said and raised his spoon in tribute.

"Hey, that's about my limit with cooking. Macy said she didn't think it was right that the women did all the cooking and cleaning and I agreed. I'm happy to cook once a week. I think we should all take turns," McCann said, hoping for Macy's approval, but by the straight face she was using he wasn't sure if she appreciated his efforts or not.

"Hold on," Marcy said. "Mark's a terrible cook. I don't want him in the kitchen. When Tala was recovering at the prepper camp, he made us Vienna sausages with peanut butter and ranch dressing on the side," she shuddered at the memory. "It was *horrible*."

They all laughed, and McCann defended him by saying, "Hey now, at least he made something."

"He can make fried egg sandwiches," Bang said. "They're pretty good."

Mark held up his hands. "Thank you, Bang. I'm fine being restricted from cooking. It's not my talent, anyway. I sure appreciate Tala's cooking, though."

They all agreed and, like most evenings, they ate together and only spoke when they needed to. They were all too engrossed in their own thoughts concerning the radio silence and newcomers to engage in routine planning. Once they finished, everyone pitched in to clean up. Then they bedded down for the evening and hoped to sleep through the night before the next day's challenge began.

With the new addition, Graham and Tala's separate bedroom became their private haven, away from the other residents. Still, when he and Tala had first begun sleeping in their own room together, he complained when she kept the door open a crack to hear the others. Then, when they'd tried to sleep with it completely closed, he just couldn't take the silence and ended up getting up in the middle of the night to check on everyone. Graham finally succumbed to leaving the door open a crack to hear the other snores he'd come so accustomed to. Those peaceful snores meant his new family's well-being throughout the night.

Dutch winked at the girl who called herself Liza. He did it to calm her nerves when she darted her eyes at him as she reached for her shotgun beneath her coat. The residents were casing them nearby. With a silent hand motion to the dogs Elsa and Frank, he *stayed* them in their place. Despite their instincts, they didn't as much as whine upon hearing horses approach at a distance.

He carefully handed Liza the jerky, and she followed his example to keep all motions open and easy. Dutch's eyes implored her to remain calm and not act out of fear lest she could get them killed.

When he thought the observers had passed after having made their assessments, he heard their retreat through the woods. He wasn't certain if anyone remained behind to watch them, but he didn't think so. All of his prior radio surveillance told him these people were good; they were surviving and seemed to be able to help others. Although admirable in their actions, Dutch was here to tell them to quit it, or they were going to get themselves killed.

His plan was to warn them, hand over the girl, and head north by himself. He didn't plan to stick around and make friends with these people.

As he sat next to Liza the crickets resumed their chirping, so he figured the watchers were long gone. Liza stared into the fire with glazed-over eyes. In Dutch's estimation she'd done pretty well today but he didn't want her to get too attached to him, just trust him enough not to flinch every time he came near her.

"Why don't you go ahead and bed down in the truck cab tonight? I'll sleep under the wagon."

She merely nodded and hustled through the cold night to the truck with a fur skin wrapped around her shoulders to protect her from the chill of the spring night. While he stirred the hot embers of the fire, Dutch heard the soft click of the cab door as Liza closed it with care.

The night was starry and the moon only a crescent. The troubled nation they once had was rambling around in Dutch's mind. The wars, religion, and simple call for equality had brought man back to the same place where he had begun—staring up at the stars with a stick in his hand and fire beneath him. Man was nothing more and nothing less than an animal with the ability to start a fire, and that made him perilous to all other creatures, but especially his fellow man.

Dutch saw no way to stop those to the south who'd take your head from your shoulders. Not believing in their ways meant death; Christ, they'd killed most of humankind, and with so few left to fight them now, all seemed lost. Perhaps he could find a place to live out his days while the planet succumbed to savages with sticks.

At dawn, Graham woke to the sound of Tala speaking in the other room. She was telling a story; he could tell by the timbre and cadence of her voice. The bedroom was darker than usual, and when he finally opened his eyes, only a soft gray light filtered in through the window.

He brushed a hand down his face and threw back the covers. In his boxer shorts and a T-shirt, he sat up and grabbed his jeans. It was a new day, and he suspected this one would come with a twist following the events of the day before.

He ambled into the kitchen, brushed his hand across the top of Bang's head, and smiled at Tala, who sat at the table recounting more of the Indian folklore she'd grown up with as a child. He headed to get his coffee and then joined her at the table.

"You've heard the one about Fire, right?" Tala asked.

Bang shook his head no.

"Long ago, Bear owned Fire, and Fire kept Bear warm throughout the year and lit his way in the dark of night. One day Bear set Fire down when he came to a great forest where acorns were scattered on the ground. Bear wandered into the forest farther and farther away from Fire as he found more and more acorns, until Fire was nearly extinguished.

"Man walked by, and the small flame of Fire begged Man to feed it, for it was nearly extinguished altogether. Man gave Fire a stick, which he placed to the north of him. Fire consumed this and grew bright. Then man set another stick to the west, and Fire grew even stronger. Man gave yet another stick, placing this one to the south of Fire, and then finally another that he set to the east. This caused Fire to burn strong, orange flames that flickered and snapped with delight. By now, Fire blazed mightily and was very pleased to have Man as a friend.

"Then one day, Bear came back to the edge of the forest, and when Fire saw Bear, he was very angry and burned white-hot. He remembered Bear was not a good friend. So he drove Bear back into the dark forest, where he now, ever after, must sleep through the winter to stay warm. And now Man owns Fire."

Graham nodded and sipped his coffee. He thought the tale was kind of an intense topic for first thing in the morning, and Bang looked shocked and upset.

"What, Buddy?" Graham asked him gently.

"So, does that mean Bear hates man for taking Fire away from him?"

Tala looked at Graham as if to say, *This one is all yours,* and she went into the bathroom without another word.

"No, Bang, Graham said. "It means Bear is a lousy friend. And Fire has a bad attitude."

"What about Man?" Bang asked.

"It wasn't Man's fault at all. He just walked by and helped Fire."

"Yeah, but now Bear is going to be mad at Man."

"Should we not help someone in need if someone else is going to be mad at us?"

Then Graham was struck with an idea to help Bang finally understand. He might not ever have this opportunity again to get through to the boy an idea that might help him understand he had no culpability in Addy's accident. He reached across the table and grasped Bang's hands to have his full attention. "Just like you helped Addy that day, Bang. No one blames you for Addy's hearing loss. You helped her when she needed it. You saved her life, Bang."

The boy visibly swallowed and blinked his eyes. His chin began to quiver and tears ran down his cheeks. Graham guided him around the table and hugged him tightly until his own shirt was soaked with the tearful regrets of the little boy.

~ ~ ~

A pair of headlights gleaming through the gray rainy day appeared in the front window. Graham saw two shadowed figures hasten toward the front door of the cabin, so he ushered Bang off into the bunkroom as Tala emerged from the bathroom.

"The guys are here," he said as he went to open the door, his voice still hoarse from the lack of warming coffee.

"I'll grab some towels; they're probably soaked through from this rain," Tala said.

"Looks like they drove the Jeep, so don't worry." Graham waited for their clomping, mud-releasing steps on the porch before he swung open the door, intent on holding the heat in as long as possible.

"Hey there. Morning," Graham said.

Dalton only nodded in a somber way, but Rick grinned as always and returned with, "What are you guys doing on this fine, rainy spring day?"

"We had enough sense to stay dry—unlike the two of you," Graham answered. "You guys want some coffee?" As he led them into the dining area, Tala had already set a second pot on and brought out the coveted sugar cookies from their hiding spot.

"Something tells me you guys aren't here for treats," Graham said.

"Where's the rest of the crew?" Dalton asked.

"They are either at your camp, in the fields, or in the barn doing their chores. Bang is still here, but he's busy in the other room," Tala said.

Dalton nodded, "We need to talk about the shots we heard yesterday."

"Okay, I know that Macy said to stay off all radio frequencies, so I didn't call it in, but last night the boys and I found a campsite."

Dalton sat down at the dining table. "Did you talk to them?"

"No. No, we didn't approach them; we just observed them from afar. From what I could tell, it's one young lady—about twenty or so—and one man."

"Provisions?" Rick asked.

"Oh, yeah; they're driving an army truck and pulling a wagon, horses . . . two dogs, too."

"Armed?" Rick asked.

Graham tried to remember the scene as it lay out beside the fire. "Yes, the lady had a shotgun nearby and one leaned against the tailgate of the truck. The man had a pistol around his waist, too."

"He didn't detect you? The dogs weren't alerted?" Dalton said.

"No. I don't think so. We were a safe distance away."

"Were they talking? Did you get any idea of their names?" Rick asked.

"No. The girl seemed to be there of her own free will, but they didn't talk much. The dogs didn't stir." Graham took a sip of his coffee and observed the two men over the rim of his cup. Dalton's jaw clenched up and down as he digested the news, and Rick stared off into space.

"Okay, what's up, guys?" Graham finally asked.

Dalton looked up at him and then looked over to Rick.

Rick began. "Well, after you guys ran off to see who the shooter was, I tuned to the local HF band. Seems someone is out to warn us to stop all transmissions. A guy named Dutch sent us a Morse code message warning us that there are . . . um . . . Headhunters to the south of us."

Graham had begun to lift his coffee again, but then set it down abruptly, causing the liquid to slosh out and create a small puddle of brown liquid on the table.

"Headhunters?" he asked, purposely hushed.

Dalton looked to see that Tala was out of the room; he didn't want to scare her, but soon all of them would have to know.

"If this guy is right, it means we're being invaded. It means our old enemy is responsible for vast genocide and they're here now to finish the job."

Graham sat back, digesting the theory. "You think the guy we saw last night is this Dutch fella?"

"Yeah," Rick said.

"And if what he says is true, we have a fight on our hands. A big one," Dalton added.

"Well, wait a minute," Graham said. "We're just now living. We've all been through hell and back, and things are finally starting to work out. It's only Tala and me with a bunch of kids here. Hell, we've got a baby on the way, Dalton," he said, surprised at the anger in his voice.

"Hey, I get that. Believe me, I do. But if they're here," Dalton said with an inner fury and shook his head, "I will decimate them. We cannot let them take it from us. I'll die first." The vehemence emanating from Dalton's eyes matched each syllable uttered.

Their eyes locked, and Graham was barely aware that Rick had spoken.

"Well, we won't know any more until we go see this guy."

"Okay, let me get ready. I'll take McCann with us," Graham said.

"All right; we'll wait in the Jeep," Rick said.

Chair legs scratched the floor's surface as they slid back, signaling that this meeting was over . . . for now.

Tala heard every word from her position in the bunkroom. She had busied Bang with folding laundry in her room, and as she put away towels, she heard their hushed voices. She didn't mean to eavesdrop, but she couldn't help but hear the fear-laced words the men spoke.

She stopped in her tracks, contemplating what it all meant. When Graham rounded the corner and found her, he knew from the fright in her eyes that she had heard.

"Come on. It's going to be fine," he said as he held his arms open to embrace her. "I'll talk to this guy. Maybe he just saw a large raiding group. Maybe he's wrong."

Tala pulled away and looked up at him. "If he's right, we're not safe here. Not the baby, not any of us. We should leave."

Graham shook his head. "Don't worry about this, Tala. It's going to be okay. You'll see. I won't let anything happen to us."

She tried to believe him, but she was too jaded from recent events. Graham retrieved his boots, touching her shoulder on his way out the door.

She watched him depart, his retreating back descending into the mist, until Bang arrived, bearing a teetering stack of awkwardly folded towels and seemingly very proud of himself for the effort.

"Thank you, Bang," Tala praised, trying to hide her fear. "You're such a big help!" Bang ran past her and out the front door into the rain to wave to Graham while Tala looked on, afraid for them all. The silver showers clouded with haze shone with two headlights backing out of the drive. She couldn't help but feel this was the beginning of something dreadful, like remembering a bad dream. She shook herself out of it, and the baby kicked as though reminding her of its presence. She put the laundry down and ran her hands down both sides of her belly. "You're fine, little one," she murmured.

"Where are they going?" Macy asked from the doorway, surprising Tala.

Tala wasn't certain what to say. She avoided making eye contact. "They've got some business to check out. We aren't sure yet."

"What are you not telling me?" Macy asked.

"Nothing, really; a guy made radio contact with Rick yesterday. They think the man at the campsite that Graham and the boys found last night might be him. They're going off to speak to him now."

"Why didn't someone tell me?" Macy asked, sounding offended.

Tala considered Macy. At sixteen, she wasn't a child anymore; she was just as capable as Mark and McCann at providing for the group, and Tala sympathized with her frustration of the double standard she often put up with from Graham.

"Macy, I don't know. Things happen fast around here, but if you ask me, you should have been told. I don't think Mark knows either, if that makes you feel any better. Where *are* Mark and your sister, anyway?"

Macy chuckled. "Who knows? It's too wet to be in the fields. They're probably wrapped up in one of the tree stands together."

"Oh, don't say that," Tala said, but she knew it was a likely scenario.

"Well, it's true. I don't even know her anymore," Macy confided, then walked out into the haze again.

Tala didn't have any advice to give. She thought it was all part of growing up too fast in this survival environment. These days they'd all done a lot of barely surviving. She was now, for all intents and purposes, married to Graham and having his child despite the viral risk. And now this new threat; she prayed they'd all make it through this, too.

"They're about another mile through the trees," Graham said over the Jeep's engine. The rain still poured, though it was not as fierce as before.

They drove as far as they could until the trail met the trees. There Rick cut the engine, and they set out on foot.

"I'm sure they know we're here by now," Graham said as he led the team. "It's just through the trees here." He couldn't get over how fast the mushrooms came up this time of year. Stepping on a large one could send you slickly flying forward if you weren't careful. The purple flower clusters of phlox blanketed treeless patches, and ferns grew green and bright, sending their little fingers out toward what meager light might be emitted through the treetops on a sunny day. This had to be his favorite time of year. As a boy he had rarely spent time at the cabin in the spring, so this was all new to him.

Typically, spring in nearby Seattle meant the bright garish reds, yellows, and blues of daffodils, tulips, and hyacinth planted in geometric shapes throughout the city. But this was spring through and through, in all its natural beauty. The moss underfoot wafted a musty smell through the forest path.

"Hey, I think we should post Rick and McCann as sentries while you and I walk in together—just in case we have any problems. Okay with you?" Dalton said.

Graham looked at McCann and he nodded, indicating that he would cover him. "Yeah, sure, but I hope it doesn't come to that," Graham said.

"You and me both, brother, but we can't be too careful. Tala would kill me if something happened to you," Dalton said to lighten the mood.

"She would—outright, even," Graham agreed.

Once they could see the clearing through the trees, Dalton stopped and pointed to two points of cover for the sentries, who peeled off from the path while Graham and Dalton continued.

As they got closer Graham could see that the wagon and truck remained parked where they had been the night before. The young woman sat between the two vehicles, her red hair a bright contrast to the gray around them. The fire had been out long ago by the rain, and a blue tarp was rigged to provide the young woman with dry shelter as she appeared to be cooking something over a portable stove.

"Do you see the guy? Or the dogs?" Dalton asked.

Graham looked around. "No, I don't."

"Let's go in. Maybe she'll tell us something. Keep your hands out in the open, and if I yell *down*, dive," Dalton warned him.

"Will do," Graham said.

As they walked into the clearing they both made sure to harden their steps in an attempt to alert their host. She looked up at Graham and then Dalton, her untrusting green eyes assessing them.

"Hi," Graham said lifting his hand.

"Hello," Liza answered. She appeared mildly frightened, but who wouldn't be in this new world when meeting a stranger?

"We heard you guys come in last night. We live close by. Do you need anything?"

"No. I don't think so," she said.

"My name is Graham, and this is Dalton." Graham took a few more steps toward her.

"Stay right there, please," she said shakily and both Dalton and Graham noticed a shotgun's barrel poking out from underneath her fur cloak. Dalton suddenly had one hand full of the back of Graham's jacket, steadily yanking him backward.

"We mean you no harm, lady," Dalton said. "We're only checking on things."

Graham had his hands up in his best no-offense mode as her eyes darted to the trees, passing left and right of them. She was getting more nervous, and that wasn't a good sign.

"How many are in your group?" Graham asked, trying to distract her. *She's looking for someone. Where's that guy and those dogs?*

"Just two," she said with a nervous smile.

"Are you guys just passing through?" Dalton asked, still holding onto the back of Graham's jacket.

"I dunno," she said, staring pointedly past them into the forest.

They both followed her line of sight and spotted Rick, who was looking none too pleased with a gag in his mouth and his hands tied behind his back as he was shoved forward by his assailant, who had a pistol aimed at his side.

"Hey!" Graham shouted, but Dalton had already drawn his weapon and pulled Graham behind him.

"We mean no harm, you asshole!" Dalton yelled.

"This is just for insurance; just like the lookouts you put up," the stranger said calmly.

"All right, you've made your point. Let him go now," Graham said.

"Let's get some answers first," Dutch said.

"Okay. What do you want to know?" Graham asked.

"You guys turned off the transmissions?"

"So, you're Dutch?" Dalton asked.

"Yes."

"Then yes, we've turned them off," Dalton answered.

"Let him go now," Graham said.

"Not so fast. How many people do you have here?" Dutch asked.

"You have a lousy way of making friends, you know that?" Dalton said.

"I'm not here to make friends."

"How about we all lower our weapons?" Graham said.

"How about you answer the question?" Dutch shot back.

"About thirty," Dalton said.

"And about half of those are children," Graham added.

"Are you guys immune to the virus?" Dutch asked.

"Yes," Graham answered, thinking it wasn't the time to elaborate on technicalities.

Dutch pulled out his pocketknife, showing Dalton and Graham he meant to cut loose Rick's ties. "Okay, I didn't mean to scare you guys. You can't be too careful these days."

Rick pulled down his gag as soon as he was able to and turned to face his attacker. Graham thought he was going to hear a stream of profanity, since Rick was quite talented in that area. Catching Dutch off guard, Rick shoved him backward by the shoulders instead.

Both men went sprawling onto the ground and, luckily, Rick had sent Dutch's gun spiraling out of reach. Graham remembered that Dutch wore a prosthesis and contemplated jumping in his defense, but Rick's arms were swinging and Dutch was doing his best to deflect each punch. Finally Dalton reached down, grabbed Rick, and dragged him up off Dutch. "That's enough!" he yelled.

Then the girl screamed as if someone had just committed murder, and Graham could tell that she wasn't well. He looked at Dutch for answers, but he lay on the ground wiping away blood from his lip and appeared to realize his young companion was in distress.

Graham walked toward her. "Hey, lady. Everything's fine. He's okay."

"Don't, Graham," Dalton warned but was too far away to yank him back again.

That's when the blast went off.

It wasn't hard for Macy to follow the Jeep's tracks through the mud. She had saddled up McCann's mare, knowing that taking his favorite horse would bug him, but that didn't matter to her. She wanted to annoy him in the way he annoyed her—the way he was taking her place because she was a girl, the way he decided she would be his without her permission.

He had tried to conquer her in his silent way. She didn't want to be owned, and she didn't want to own anyone else. Your heart hurts terribly when you lose someone you're apt to claim possession of, and she never wanted to go through that again. Not ever.

Macy followed the Jeep tracks through the rain, wearing a dove-colored Stetson hat to shield her from the shower. The earth smelled clean and new, and she thought that shouldn't be the case; it should cease to smell fresh after all of the deaths, and it should cease to nurture tender green sprouts. The sky should never turn blue, yet she could already see a clearing in the clouds, and she thought it a betrayal to all she'd loved and lost.

Sheriff appeared out of nowhere and trotted alongside Macy, as he often did. One minute he wasn't there and the next he was. He was her companion, but she didn't own him; Sheriff owned himself, and everyone knew it. She figured he just liked her best of all his humans, or perhaps he knew she was doing something she shouldn't, and he wanted to go along to watch over her. In any event, she was thankful for his presence. He looked up at her occasionally, with his tongue lolling out; the smell of his damp fur wafted up to her nose.

"You smell, my friend," she said, and Sheriff seemed offended. He cut his eyes away from her as though knowing exactly what her words meant.

Macy led the horse through the new growth of a meadow toward the farthest tree line, where she spotted the Jeep she'd been stalking.

When they reached the empty vehicle, Sheriff sniffed at the boot prints and the telling mark of Graham's cane that led into the forest.

"That's almost too easy to follow," Macy whispered as she ducked under low-hanging branches. Sheriff ran up ahead to lead the way as he followed their scent. He stopped suddenly, and Macy watched as a sense of confusion crossed him. He looked first north, then west and east, and then he turned to look at her astride the horse, as if needing her counsel for their next course of action.

"What do you think, Sheriff? Where'd they go?"

He sat on his haunches, waiting for a cue from Macy.

"Hmmm," Macy said, not certain of what this meant.

Then Sheriff's ears perked toward the east, and his muzzle followed. He stood and sniffed, then shot her a look before he began an easterly trot in tentative exploration. Something was up; Macy could tell by his actions.

It wasn't long before they came upon a scene she never thought she would witness.

Sheriff's ominous growl unnerved her as he lowered himself to his haunches, waiting to attack. The two other dogs did the same before their prey. McCann sat bound and gagged against a pine trunk with pale attack dogs guarding their prisoner.

"What the heck happened to you?" Macy said, instinctively knowing to keep her voice low. McCann's eyes implored her to leave as he jerked his head to the right. Macy surveyed her surroundings for the others, her hand on the pistol grip of her .45 as she dismounted the mare. One of the dogs turned to her despite Sheriff's warnings, and McCann shook his head, causing the other dog to turn on him and bark a warning an inch from his face.

"Git!" Macy yelled and then she heard the shrill scream of a woman in distress, followed by a massive explosion. Instantly Macy sunk to a crouch against the pine-needled blanket and raised her pistol. When she looked back, both guard dogs were gone and McCann looked at her with terrified concern. She ran to him and crouched at his side. With her unsheathed knife she tore through the bindings around his wrists, and while she went to work on his ankle bindings, he ripped down the gag and yelled at her, "Get out of here! Go, Macy—*now!*"

"Shut up," she said as she continued to cut at the binding.

He reached and took her weapon from her. "I mean it, Macy; get the hell out of here!"

"No," she said. "Where's Graham?"

He shook his head and blew an exasperated breath at her. "You—" he cut himself off and turned toward the right while pulling her behind him and using the next tree as a shield. They inched their way toward what Macy guessed was the location of the others.

The familiar click of Macy's .45 told her McCann had pulled back the hammer of her pistol, getting ready to fire. He still held onto her shirt by her waist with a tight grip, holding her close to his back. She shoved his hand away, knowing he'd get hurt if was he partially impaired by her presence. Why did he have to worry about her? She could take care of herself.

"Stop it," she said, slapping his hand away.

"Stay right behind me, Macy. I mean it, or I'll tie you up," he warned.

She huffed, "Like hell."

"Shhh," he said.

Macy heard whimpering and turned to see that Sheriff had followed the two at a crouch. She reached back and held his collar, pulling him to her side to keep him out of McCann's way. She noticed the horse had backed up several yards from her previous position. Everything had happened so fast that Macy hadn't thought about how lucky it was that McCann's mare hadn't tried to flee and trample her in the process.

There were angry voices, though neither McCann nor Macy could hear specifically what they were saying.

"Macy, please stay right here," McCann said, his brown eyes pleading with her to obey him. The vibration of his racing heartbeat trembled his shirt collar.

"No," she whispered, a quiet defiance this time.

He looked away from her. "Stay close, then."

She followed as they scurried another ten feet closer to the angry voices to get a look at the chaotic scene.

"Oh, son of a bitch!" Rick's voice yelled in agony. Macy leaned around McCann to see who was hurt. Her pulse raced and her heart thundered inside her chest.

She saw a stranger sitting up to the left of Dalton and Rick. Rick was holding his shin, and blood was spreading over his hands. She looked farther and saw Graham lying prone, face down on the ground. McCann must have seen him, too, and he began to step forward, but Macy pulled him back when she noticed the stranger holding his hand up to someone farther away. A woman with flaming red hair stood up, screaming, between a truck and a horse wagon. A shotgun fell to the ground, and the young woman turned and fled. The unknown man chased after her, shouting, "Liza!"

Macy then pushed McCann from behind and they both entered the clearing with Sheriff by their side. "Graham?" Macy called and ran to him. She barely noticed all the blood in her peripheral vision as she passed Rick, where Dalton was trying to stem the crimson flow from his leg.

"Graham!" she yelled again as she skidded to her knees before him, ruining newly sprouted spring growth beneath her. McCann's boots appeared beside her. Although no blood puddled around Graham, she was afraid to touch him. Almost crying, she grabbed his shoulder; McCann reached down and helped her turn him to his side.

"Graham?" she asked again and saw where the rock had hit him — or, rather, where his forehead had landed on the rock. McCann checked for breathing. He pushed Macy out of the way and opened the front of Graham's jacket, then leaned down to his face, turning his head and listening.

"Is he okay? Is he hit?" Dalton asked.

"Oh, Jesus!" Rick yelled.

"Is he breathing?" Macy asked, waiting for the answer. McCann's brown eyes looked toward Graham's chest as he listened.

It was torture, this waiting.

"Yes," he said finally.

McCann pulled away, sat back, and pushed Graham's hair from his forehead, his hand coming away damp with blood. He further parted Graham's hair and peered down at the minor split in his scalp. "I think he's just knocked out. We should get him to Clarisse. He could have swelling."

McCann pushed Macy back again as he looked for any other signs of injury that Graham might have. He'd been through the ringer already last winter, and now this.

Dalton was busy putting pressure on Rick's wounds. Most of the shot had been absorbed by the ground, but Rick had caught a partial scatter to the lower leg above his boot line.

"Is Graham okay?" Dalton's insistent voice beckoned.

"He's got a head injury; it's hard to say. He's breathing, but we need to get him to Clarisse. How's Rick?" McCann asked.

Before Dalton could answer, McCann placed his fingers in his mouth and whistled a loud looping sound toward the forest, and his mare obediently appeared.

"Rick will be okay; it's a flesh wound. We can take the Jeep," Dalton offered.

"I'm getting him out of here before that guy gets back here. Macy, climb up," he demanded, holding out his entwined hands for a step hold onto the horse.

She glanced at Rick and Dalton and back to McCann. She didn't want to obey, but knew McCann was right. She placed her right hand on McCann's shoulder, his jacket damp from the rain but strong and unyielding. With her muddy right boot placed in his outstretched hands, she sprung up into the air and looped her left leg over the back end of the mare. Dalton came over and, together, the two men lifted Graham's unconscious form up and over the center saddle, Macy holding him level.

"Rick's gotta come, too!" she said. "Look at all the blood."

"McCann will help him hike through the woods to the Jeep," Dalton said. "I'll stay and have a word with our new neighbor. That girl has some issues, and he needs to explain why. Macy, go now. I'll be right behind you. Go straight to Clarisse. Tala doesn't need to know for now."

Macy nodded, and the rain began again as the mare ambled forward with its load. She held the reins, but the horse seemed to know where she was going and trotted gently toward the preppers' camp with McCann's orders; Macy was a mere passenger. She blew out a frustrated breath because—again—McCann was owning her.

She ran, stumbling several times, and finally fell to the wet, uneven ground, muddy and torn. The shot still rang in her ears, the one from before and the one from just now, bringing it all back. Blood appeared vibrant red in her mind as a man toppled over.

She had run then, as she was running now, blindly into the forest, where she'd hoped the memories would not follow, but it was far too late. They were here now, surrounding her.

One minute everything was fine, then the men were fighting, and their voices grew even louder until they were on the ground swinging at one another. She fired out of terror and, not knowing the fate of the stranger, she could only run. She ran until the bright and dull shades of green blended and flowed beside her.

~ ~ ~

Dutch followed Liza but didn't try to catch her; she needed to tire herself out. He kept track of where she was going and hoped she didn't fall off a cliff. He knew there was trouble with her. She was damaged; he'd seen it before in Afghanistan as they'd rescued women from captivity. They were terrified of any man; even handing water or food was met with a flinch and a frightened stare. He saw this same behavior in this girl, the way she flinched when he'd accidentally brush against her when handing her something. Or the way she never looked him in the eyes and jumped at any loud sound . . . and not trusting him with her name. Someone had done this to her. It made Dutch sick to think about it.

Liza wasn't any different from his buddies who were burdened with awful memories of war, and he knew he had to let her ride it out. She needed to be exhausted before he could help her. So he watched and kept his distance. It was then he realized she was his responsibility after all; she wasn't ready for other people yet. He needed to help make her whole again before he could leave her here alone . . . if they would even have her now.

Dutch tracked Liza as she fled. She was slowing down; he knew she'd be exhausted soon and her legs would give out. The deep tracks led the way through the muddy earth where, on occasion, he could see her handprints, too. *Not long now*, he thought. *She'll hit the ground soon.* And then he came upon her, curled around her herself, her red hair wildly strewn in a crown about her as she sobbed in great heaves while her breath tried to catch up with her.

He approached carefully, toward her barricaded back, which harbored her broken but beating heart. She was torn and lost; he'd seen it but didn't know how badly until today. She was strong, but no one is invincible.

He knelt down beside her and gently said, "Liza?"

She curled herself up tighter.

"Liza," Dutch said again, reaching out a hand to stroke her temple.

She shot her ivy-green eyes at him with terror. She jerked away from his hand until she could see through the fog. His hand remained in a hover, waiting for her permission.

Knowing now that it was him, she closed her eyes and cried more softly.

It was enough of an invitation, and Dutch brushed her hair away from her face. "It's okay, Liza. Everything is going to be okay. I won't let anything happen to you."

"Did I . . . did I . . . kill him?" she choked between ragged breaths.

"No."

As Liza cried tears of relief, Dutch lifted her head onto his lap and stroked her vibrant hair. She trembled in his grasp, her soul wounded by this life. She tried to speak between sobs, so he bent low to hear her words.

"My name . . . is Lucy."

Macy found once herself again carting an unconscious Graham to get aid. She held her hat over him as much as she could and checked the scalp wound frequently. His scalp poured blood in a stream. She was suddenly glad there was no snow on the ground, remembering how bright blood shows in contrast against the white.

The river's roar neared; she would soon be in the preppers' camp. She resisted the urge to push the horse faster, knowing she needed to keep Graham stable more than she needed speed. The horse crossed the bridge with ease, and Macy peered around, wondering where Sheriff had gotten off to; she hoped he wasn't fighting for his life against the other two dogs. She also hoped Tala wasn't out in the woods to see them like this—Graham unconscious and her carrying him away. It felt like a betrayal, and she resented being left to deceive Tala.

Soon they reached the camp, and Steven, after a double take, ran up to her side.

"What the hell happened?"

"There was a shot," Macy began.

"He's shot?" Steven asked.

"No, Graham fell. *Rick's* shot," she said, regretting her words right away.

"Rick?"

"Yes, but it's not bad. They're coming."

"Again, what the hell happened?" Steven asked, but then ignored her when she tried to answer; instead he yelled, "Clarisse!"

Sam came to help them, and Macy again attempted an explanation as Steven began to pull Graham from the saddle.

"Someone fired a shotgun, and Graham dove down, hitting his head on a rock, and some of the pellets struck Rick in the leg. But he's fine. McCann is bringing him in with the Jeep."

"Okay, I think I get it," Steven said. By the time he and Sam had a hold of the unconscious body and turned it over, Graham had started to moan. Blood was everywhere, his face covered in it. He began to move, bringing his arm up to his head sleepily. When he pulled his hand away, it was dripping with gore. Macy turned her gaze away as she descended the mount. Taking the reins, she looked for a place to tie them when she heard Clarisse.

Steven went into medic mode, looking into Graham's eyes and calling out medical details and jargon to Clarisse. They made little sense to Macy, but when they took Graham away she knew he'd be okay. As she tied McCann's horse to a slender pine where she would be out of most of the rain, she realized the mare would need a wipe-down and a drink. She was walking through the mist to retrieve a cloth and some water from the tank to clean her off when Sam intercepted her.

"Are you okay, Macy?" he said, placing a cautious hand on her shoulder as he gave her a once-over. Blood stained her slacks and jacket where she had held onto Graham.

"Yes, I'm fine, Sam," she assured him, standing a little taller. He looked as if he doubted her words, and she wasn't sure why.

"What happened out there? Do I need to go help?" Sam asked.

"I think things are fine now; Dalton and McCann have it under control. I don't really know what happened. I came up and found McCann tied up with two dogs guarding him. Then we heard a shot, and when we got there some lady ran off through the woods and Graham was lying there . . ." she began to choke up, remembering the scene.

Sam pulled her to him.

"It's okay, Macy. He's going to be fine. He was just knocked out. It's only a scalp wound, and they bleed a lot, which makes it look worse than it is. He's awake now and pissed off, but he's fine," Sam soothed her.

He took the bucket of water from her hands. Together they washed the blood from the mare's chestnut hide until the water ran clear; then they let her drink fresh water. Macy relayed all she knew from the scene until the rumble of Dalton's Jeep reverberated through the quiet.

Steven came out and relayed to Clarisse what was wrong with Rick, as if he was only a body instead of his best friend.

"Will you knock it off?" Rick snarled. Steven ignored any utterance from the patient, however, and threatened him with a tetanus shot in the ass if he didn't shut up.

Macy watched their back-and-forth with amusement until she saw McCann staring at her in the distance; she cut her eyes away and went back to caring for his horse.

When McCann approached her, Sam went to help with Rick. Macy still didn't look at McCann, continuing to dry the horse instead.

"Why did you follow us, Macy?" McCann asked. He stood too close to her.

"I wasn't following you," she lied.

McCann waited a minute beside her, and she felt him watching her hand stroke the horse.

"Yes you were."

"I'm going to go and let Tala know what happened," she whispered.

He clasped her wrist in midstroke. "Macy," he said, gently pulling the rag from her grasp. He was shaking, and she wasn't sure what that meant.

"I'm fine, McCann," she said, pulling away, but he wouldn't let her. Instead he pulled her toward him and she relented with begrudging reluctance.

His raspy voice whispered into her ear as he held her close. "I can't let anything happen to you."

Macy's eyes widened. She was all too aware of his closeness and though she wanted someone to hold her like this, she didn't ever want to risk having her heart broken by losing someone else she loved. She placed her hands on his strong arms and pushed herself away from him.

"I'm not yours, McCann." She turned from him as one corner of his mouth bent upward.

He pulled her toward his chest again, despite her resistance, and whispered, "I don't want to own you, Macy. I just want you by my side, standing beside me. Only a man with a death wish would ever try to possess you." He then quickly released her.

She started to lead the horse away by the reins and turned to see if McCann was still watching her. He was, and she wasn't certain anymore if having him close annoyed her or if she'd just made a truce . . . of sorts.

With Dalton on one side and McCann on the other, they managed to get Rick to the Jeep—after stopping twice to rewrap his calf. Dalton knew buckshot to the shin must hurt terribly, but at least it wasn't life threatening. He would just have to hear Rick complain like a pansy for a while.

"You sure you don't want to come with us?" McCann asked.

"No, get him in. I'll walk back. That girl might need to be looked at, too."

"I'll come back after I drop off Rick," McCann had said.

"Good idea," Dalton replied. In the back of his mind, he was a bit jealous of Rick at the moment because he'd at least be in the vicinity of Clarisse soon. Being near her was something Dalton tried to arrange on a daily basis, despite the way their lives were now.

He tapped the truck's door, and when McCann took off, he double-timed it back to Dutch's camp. Although he thought Dutch's tactics were flawed, he didn't think the guy was bad unless it turned out he had been abusing the girl. If that was the case, Dalton didn't care what the guy had witnessed; he'd grab the girl and send Dutch on his way. Hopefully it wouldn't come to that.

On his approach he saw the man carrying the young woman through the rain. Her arm held him tight across the neck and her damp red hair hung down in ringlets across his arm.

"She okay?" Dalton called.

"Yeah. She's shaken up, but she's okay," Dutch said as he came into camp. He sat her down in the fur-lined chair she had fled from earlier, which had partially been covered with a tarp to cast out the rain.

Dalton knelt by her side. She shivered and her lips trembled. "Are you all right, Miss?" he asked. She flicked her eyes up at Dutch without answering. Dutch wrapped another blanket around her and picked up the shotgun she'd dropped before. Dalton watched as he wiped off the dirt and checked the load.

"I want to talk to you . . . in private," Dalton said as he stood up.

Dutch nodded, telling Lucy, "Stay here. I'll be right back."

A short distance away, Dalton waited for Dutch to catch up. He contemplated losing his cool but knew that wouldn't be good for the girl, considering how she'd reacted before. With his hands on his hips, he asked the man in an angry but controlled voice, "Do you mind telling me what the hell just happened here?"

By all appearances, Dutch seemed calm, and he didn't strike Dalton as a bad sort—meaning, he didn't think the guy had harmed the girl himself. But Dutch certainly hadn't given them the best impression. His behavior with Rick had been unsettling, but it was something Dalton would have done himself if the roles had been reversed. Dutch had calculated that they were coming in to see him; he didn't know what kind of people they were, and he took precautions to keep himself and the girl safe from them. These actions were warranted in the world they lived in now. Anyone with a tactical mind would have done the same. Dalton felt it was his own fault for not anticipating this, but he set up sentry guards himself and, given Dutch's actions, he considered him an equal.

Having Rick knock the crap out of Dutch was also predictable. Rick was humorless when humiliated; Dalton felt the blame and knew he should have stopped his buddy's attack.

What wasn't expected was the girl's reaction, and Dalton was afraid he knew the answer as to why she behaved the way she did. He just hoped Dutch wasn't the one who'd abused her.

"I think she had a flashback," Dutch explained and looked Dalton in the eye. "She's just a kid. She works hard, but she's skittish.

I came upon her fleeing from the invaders. She's been traumatized; I don't know to what extent." He shook his head.

"She ever done anything like this before?" Dalton asked.

"No. She's quiet. She was scared to death when I first found her. It's taken weeks for her to even look at me straight. She only just told me her name—Lucy. It wasn't her fault; I shouldn't have set her up with the shotgun. We haven't been around anyone else. I had no idea she'd react that way."

"You're not *with* her, right?" Dalton had to ask. He could see right away that Dutch was offended at even the suggestion.

"I could be her *father*, man. *Hell*, no! She's a girl, maybe twenty. And I'm almost fifty."

Dalton nodded, relieved at his answer. "Look, besides her, we have a lot to talk about. Why don't you two come back to camp with me? I have a doctor who can take a look at her and make sure she's okay. Then we can talk about these invaders and decide what to do." At that time, McCann came into the clearing, heading their way.

"I don't know where my dogs ran off to, and I'm not leaving my provisions unguarded here," Dutch said. "My only task was to warn you guys, drop her off, and be on my way. I've done that, and I'll be leaving as soon as she's taken care of."

"You mean you're leaving her here with us?" Dalton asked.

"Yeah, if you'll have her. She really is a good worker; she's just a little traumatized," Dutch explained.

"Don't you think that's up to her?" McCann asked once he caught on to the gist of their conversation. Dalton could tell the kid didn't much like this guy's style.

"She's not mine. I only found her. Or rather, she found me, fleeing for her life only a few weeks ago. I'm a loner, and she needs other people her own age to be around," Dutch said.

"All right; let's have McCann, here, take her back to our camp. She can stay the night with Clarisse after she's looked at. We'll figure out her living arrangements later. McCann, have Sam and Reuben come back with you."

"I have to take care of my own. I'll send them out, but then I'm checking on Graham and getting him home. You need to make the girl understand it's okay to come with me, though," McCann said.

Dalton caught his meaning that Dutch was the only one she trusted and the thought that this might be a more difficult transition than he'd anticipated crossed his mind. The girl eyed them with a distrustful glare, even now balled up on her chair, hugging her legs. She was a little thing, and Dalton felt the hollow in his stomach knowing what she must have endured at the hands of the jihadists.

Dutch cleared his throat. "Let me talk to her first. Wait here."

He walked away, and Dalton wasn't sure if he was doing the right thing by offering the girl shelter away from someone she trusted. Sometimes when you're dealing with a wounded animal, the best thing to do is let it be and wait for it to come to you. Unfortunately, it didn't appear to him that Dutch had waiting on his mind. He seemed sufficiently spooked by what he had discovered to the south and did not intend to stick around for the girl to get comfortable with her new community. Even now, as Dutch knelt down to her level in the chair, Lucy was shaking her head in disapproval of the idea.

She began to cry again, wiping at her tears with her sleeve. Dutch stroked the back of her head while he reassured her she would be safe. She didn't seem convinced.

When Dutch finally motioned for McCann to approach, both men walked toward her. Dalton wanted to let her know himself that she would be safe at their camp.

"This is McCann. He's going to take you to their camp. They have a doctor who can see to you," Dutch explained to her.

Dalton knelt down and faced Lucy's tear-streaked face before McCann stepped forward.

"Hi, I'm Dalton. I lead our camp, and this is McCann. He lives nearby, in Graham's camp. He's going to take you to my camp for the night. You'll stay with our doctor Clarisse. She's a really nice lady, and you'll be fed, have a clean shower, and a warm bed for the night. No one will bother you; I promise you that, Lucy.

She shot her terrified eyes at Dutch, realizing that he had told Dalton her name.

"It's nice to meet you," Dalton said. He held his hand out to Lucy, and she took it tentatively. Dutch placed the skinned hide she'd adopted for her own around her shoulders, and McCann led the way to the Jeep. She followed behind him, and Dalton watched as she turned every few feet to look behind her.

"I'll see you tomorrow, Lucy," Dutch said.

She nodded and turned to catch up to McCann.

"It's not that bad," Graham assured Tala when she caught a glimpse of him. Macy had already warned her, so she had had a little time to prepare before McCann brought Graham back to camp. Tala immediately pulled him into their bedroom, where she could talk to him without the others hearing.

"It's only a few stitches," he explained, but Tala's expression killed him. Suddenly she looked petrified, as if she knew this thin veil of safety was all that stood between her, their unborn child, and the hell they'd all known before.

Graham hated it. He'd do anything to have Tala feel secure in his arms, always. This life was harsh and yes, he'd been lucky today. Despite the bump and scalp wound, he'd been damn lucky in fact. Rick was the one that got the spray of buckshot, even though that was a little blow and not likely to cause any lasting problems. He was probably putting up with his own wife about now, too; Graham smiled at the thought.

"What is so funny?" Tala asked as she held an icepack on Graham's head, as Clarisse had advised.

"Rick. His wife is probably giving him hell about now."

"I still don't see why that's funny."

"You would if you were me."

She pinched him and he yelled, "Ouch!" more out of shock than the pain.

She held up her finger to him. "Don't make light of what happened today. Don't you dare." Graham could see that she was only barely keeping it together as her eyes pooled with tears.

"Tala," he took her arm down and pulled her close to him. She was pissed, but he knew the anger came from worry more than anything else. "I fully admit I was lucky as hell today. I'm sorry; I'm not making fun of the danger. I'm just thankful it wasn't worse."

"You can only get lucky a few times, Graham, before it catches up with you."

"Hey, you have to understand something; I don't take chances. I walked toward her to try to calm her down. I didn't know she was unstable. I didn't for a minute think she'd shoot at us. I don't think she was even aiming; the shotgun just went off. I think she's been through a lot. She's young, and Dalton said they were going to take care of her. He said Dutch got a hold of her after she'd been traumatized." Graham ran his hand down her spine knowing all too well that it was Tala herself who had only recently almost succumbed to men who were bent on the same sort of torture.

"It wasn't her fault," he repeated in a whisper. "I can only imagine what they put her through. When the other guys were arguing she flipped and then the shotgun went off. She's going to be okay now. Clarisse is monitoring her, and she'll be living with them for now," he said as his hand widened around Tala's hip.

Tala relaxed in his arms and leaned her head into the crook of his neck. He cradled her belly with his palm and whispered into her ear as she sat in his lap on the bed that had become theirs. "I love you, Tala, but you need to know I have every faith that you're strong enough to carry on if something were ever to happen to me—that you would take the rest of the group and go with Dalton. Promise me," he said, caressing her side and kissing her neck.

"No," Tala said. Another tear dropped, and she clutched Graham's shirt with both hands. "I won't ever leave here without you, so *don't* get yourself killed."

There was no arguing with Tala when she was defiant like this. Once she set her mind on something, that was that, and Graham knew of only one infallible way, without argument, to reassure her in silence that he loved her and would do anything to protect her.

"It was them. I was in Afghanistan," Dutch explained. "I have no doubts who they are. I monitored the radios. My dad was an old HAM radio operator, and he kept all the equipment. I started listening in one day—for background noise, more than anything else, after everyone in town passed on.

"The broadcast was mostly static in the beginning, a few auto transmissions and repeaters that were never turned off; then one day I heard your Morse transmission. I've known code since I was a kid, because of my dad. I deciphered yours, and since the message was on a beacon, I wasn't sure if you guys were really here. The day I convinced myself to contact you back, I heard their traffic over the shortwave.

"After that, I didn't even attempt a broadcast. I listened in to find out where they were and rode two days north to see what I hoped hadn't happened. Unfortunately, the people I saw were no different from the enemy we fought for years in the desert. They're here now. There's no mistaking that."

Dutch's words hung in the air as a nightmare come true. What they'd all suspected had now became real, ominous—heinous.

The rain had picked up to a steady rhythm against the blue tarp and filled the silence as Dalton silently hoped that Dutch was mistaken. Steven looked at him like he was speaking Swahili, while Sam sat back and pondered the situation. To Dalton they all appeared utterly defeated, and this wasn't good. They needed to fight them. They needed to wipe them from their soil, make them pay for all the lives they'd taken. Send them back to their God on a fast track—and without the virgins.

"How many and what kind of weapons are they packing?" Sam asked.

Dutch shook his head in defeat before he answered, "*Ours*, man. They're packing *our* weapons, driving *our* trucks on *our* land, and there's a lot of them. I saw at least two or three hundred, and that's just here. I'm sure they're in every major port by now. They did this to us, and we lost. There's no fighting them now. I'm going north; you ought to do the same. Anyone they find they'll either enslave or kill outright. I've seen it."

How did you find Lucy?" Steven asked.

"Lucy found me. I think she escaped from capture. She's never wanted to talk about it, but she was running like hell through the woods that night and ran right into me. She was covered in someone else's blood. I hate to think of what happened to her, but she's a lot better than she was—despite what happened here today. I hope you guys will give her a chance."

"That's not a problem, Dutch. We'll give her a fair chance. What we need to discuss is how we can get these bastards off our soil," Dalton said.

"Like I said, there's too many of them. I'm going north to Canada. If and when we do have enough numbers to do something about it, I'm all in; until then, I'm becoming a Canadian."

"That doesn't sit well with me," Dalton said with more venom than he intended.

A moment passed before Sam filled the tension with a more pressing question. "Have you monitored their conversations on the radio since then? Have they talked about their plans?"

"Yeah," Dutch said, "more of the same; mostly in Arabic, some of which I picked up in my last employment. *Taking the land from the infidels. Removing the scourge from sea to sea.* They're burning any and all monuments, churches . . . everything. It's sick. I'm no coward, man," he directed his comment at Dalton, "but there's no fighting that. We don't have enough men or weapons. The writing's on the wall. They won, we lost."

Dalton couldn't take Dutch's defeatist attitude. He stood and yelled, "That's bullshit! During the revolution we were outnumbered. We didn't give up then. We didn't let the British win. We're no different now. There's got to be a way."

"This isn't the revolution, and their numbers are greater now, Dalton. Believe me, if there's a way, I'm all for it. If you've got a plan, let's work it."

"No one followed you here, right?" Sam asked.

"No, I don't think so, but I'm telling you, I think you have a week at the most. They're coming, and borders are no obstacle for them. We saw it in the Middle East. Once they declared a caliphate there, nothing held them back. We were too fucking lackadaisical in our pansy-ass limited airstrike shit. No, our own government had as much to do with our downfall as they did. What a fucking waste," Dutch said.

"So they used the virus to kill us all, and then waited?" Steven asked, trying to summarize the events.

"I think so, man," Dutch nodded solemnly.

"There were early, but unsubstantiated, reports that China weaponized H5N1 and then sold it to the highest bidder. They did anything it took to stick it to the United States. Guess we know who won the auction, though I don't think China celebrated for long. It backfired on them and everyone started dying off before we could even begin to investigate," Dalton said.

"We need to take a scouting trip and see how far they've come. Get our people out of harm's way and then make a plan of attack," Sam said.

"Yeah, I agree. Dutch, can you stay a while with us and lead us to where you saw them last so we can get an idea of their numbers and their location?"

Dutch shook his head, and Dalton knew this would be a battle.

"Dalton, I am making my way north. I'm not sticking around here. If you guys come up with some grand idea to wipe them all out at once, let me know. I'm just passing through and giving you guys the warning along the way," Dutch said.

"That's it? You're dropping a bomb on us and leaving? Like, *deal with it*? Like it or not, you're an American, and right now we're in short supply of those—in case you haven't noticed. We need you here with us to fight these bastards," Steven said.

Dalton realized the conversation could easily get out of control, and he needed to pull everyone together. Steven was typically mild-mannered, but even he was getting pretty pissed off.

"I agree with Sam. We need to form a scout team and check these guys out. Just three or four of us; I don't want to leave our people undefended in case things go the wrong way. Dutch, we could really use you, but I won't stand in your way if you're leaving. Thanks for the warning." Dalton stood and signaled that the meeting was adjourned. They'd gotten about all they could from Dutch, and it seemed pretty clear that he wasn't willing to give them anymore. There was no sense in fighting over it.

"Lucy will be fine with us," Sam said. "Don't worry about her."

"Thanks," Dutch said and shook Sam's hand.

"Are you going to head out?" Dalton asked him as the others rose to depart.

"I'll head out in the morning."

"Well, it was nice meeting you, Dutch, and good luck out there." Dalton shook the man's hand with a firm grip.

"You're going to leave the girl without saying good-bye to her?" Steven asked.

"Steven," Dalton said as a warning. "Let the man go. We all have our own decisions to make."

"It's all right," Dutch answered. "She's not mine. She doesn't belong to me, but I will come by tomorrow on my way out and bring her a few things."

"Why don't you at least stay until we get back? You could help keep an eye on things," Steven suggested.

"I'll think about it."

Dalton nodded, thinking, *At least he considered Steven's suggestion.* He then led the others back into the rain with new troubles on their minds and a plan beginning to form.

It was dark, but he could see their shadows coming. "Where have you guys been?" McCann asked Mark and Marcy as they passed the newly erected stables on their way to the cabin.

Mark stopped so suddenly that Marcy ran into his back. He hadn't expected McCann to be waiting for them there. "We were . . . hanging out," he said, stumbling over his words.

"Where?" McCann didn't even try to hide his anger.

"What's with you?" Marcy challenged.

"I was getting ready to saddle up and come find you two. Do you even know what's happened today?" McCann yelled.

"What? What happened?" Mark asked.

"While you two were out screwing around, Graham nearly got shot and instead fell and hit his head pretty bad. Rick *did* get shot, taking a graze to his leg. If it wasn't for Macy, I might be dead, and you two weren't even around here to help out when we needed you." He was surprised at his own anger and jerked when he felt Macy's soft touch on his arm behind him, trying to calm him down.

"Is Graham all right?" Mark asked.

McCann took a deep breath and tried for a calmer tone. "Yeah. He's taking it easy with Tala. He's had a rough day."

"We decided to stay out here and give them some time to themselves for a while," Macy added.

"Have you guys seen Sheriff?" Bang asked from behind Macy.

Mark ignored Bang's question. "What happened? Who nearly shot Graham?"

McCann didn't want to explain it. He was frustrated with them and had no intentions of trying to make them feel better. He took a deep breath of the moist night air and said, "Come on, Bang, let's go see if we can find Sheriff." He'd already saddled Mosey to find the missing teens earlier. He mounted up and reached down to Bang, grabbing him and pulling him up onto the back of the saddle.

"Don't be out long," Macy said to him, trying to smile.

McCann nodded at her and cut his eyes away from Mark and Marcy.

"I'll explain," Macy said to the pair as he trotted away.

"McCann's really pissed," Marcy said.

"You'd be, too," Macy shot back, and McCann took some satisfaction from her tone; at least she seemed to be on his side with this one. As McCann and Bang rode through the starry night, Macy's voice trailed off.

"Is Graham going to be okay?" Bang asked timidly.

"Yeah, buddy, he's fine. He was knocked out for a while, and scalp cuts bleed a lot, but he's going to be fine."

"Good. I don't want anything to happen to him. I don't know where I'd go if he died," Bang said.

McCann led the horse in silence, thinking about what to say to Bang. Things were different these days, and outright lying just wasn't the right thing to do to a little boy in these times. There was no reassuring him completely; sadly, at five, Bang already knew that.

"Bang, you know that if something ever happened to Graham, I would take care of you, right? We're a family now. And if I am also gone and Tala is gone"—he tried to put it tactfully—"Dalton would take you. But you're not an ordinary kid, Bang." He laughed and patted Bang on the knee behind him. "You've got skills. You can take care of yourself. I've seen you snare a rabbit, gut it, skin it, and roast it over a fire pit you made yourself, all in less than an hour. There's not much more to taking care of yourself if you can hunt and feed yourself."

"Would you take care of Macy if something happened to me?" Bang asked him.

McCann cleared his throat. He knew how close Macy and Bang were. They were more siblings than Macy was a sister to Marcy. "Macy can take care of herself, too."

"No. She needs me. She gets sad sometimes, and lonely," Bang revealed.

"We all do, buddy; but yeah, I'd take care of her," McCann said. He pulled out another toothpick to chew on while he stared through the moonlight ahead of them. They heard a distant howl, which ended their conversation, and McCann nudged Mosey with his heels enough to get him to speed up a little from his normal pace.

"Sheriff!" Bang called out while McCann whistled long and low, hoping to catch the dog's attention. It wasn't like Sheriff to run off without showing back up around dinnertime, and even McCann was beginning to worry.

"Lucy," Clarisse called to her from outside the shower stalls. "You can change into these scrubs I'm putting on the chair here," she said.

"Okay, Clarisse, thank you," Lucy called back through the steam.

Clarisse had been horrified when McCann brought Lucy into camp. At first she was upset to know the shooter was coming in to stay with them, but after McCann explained what he thought the girl's circumstances were she understood. Lucy was a small, timid thing, and Clarisse's heart went out to her. Everyone could see for themselves that the girl was trying to cope with some nightmare, that she was clearly in shock from some remembered trauma. She'd have to get over her terror, however, or she'd never survive in this world; and they couldn't afford her taking a life by accident.

It took a little coaxing, but after Lucy had showered and changed Clarisse was able to get the girl to tell her what had happened to her.

~ ~ ~

She was living near Spokane when the invaders captured her. They nearly killed her when she was asked to translate a few words in Arabic, and she hadn't a clue what they were.

The hand that had clenched her hard by the back of her hair had pulled her head back to expose her throat to the sharp blade of a knife, which was meant to spill her blood. Another hand blocked the strike at the last second; a man with dark olive skin pulled the other man away. He grabbed handfuls of her striking red hair and pulled her hard against him. In broken English, he asked her if she was a virgin. She cried, knowing she might be saved, if only for a short and torturous time. She shook her head "no," not wanting to give them the satisfaction of knowing she was.

The olive-skinned man paused for a moment and searched her face as if making a decision. He then shoved her to the ground and made her kneel before him; her hands were still tied behind her back. She had guessed he was about to take her head then and there, but instead he robed her in black from head to toe, even covering her face. Then he tied a rope around her neck and connected her to the back of his vehicle. She was made to follow on foot alongside other weeping prisoners. She suspected they were mostly young girls and their cries were only the beginning of the nightmare to come.

She'd fallen many times while bumping into other prisoners, but she somehow found the strength to stand and move rather than be dragged along the hard road. She could barely see through the slits in the head covering.

After they'd stopped later that night, she was separated from the others. She could barely walk, and they half-dragged her down a hall and brought her to what looked like an empty hotel room. She didn't know where she was or how far they'd traveled, only that men yelled in strange languages, people screamed for mercy, and she was terrified. The smell of blood was everywhere. These men were animals in their butchery, and Lucy had no idea how long her death might be postponed; she could die at any given moment, and each second seemed like borrowed time.

Finally she was shoved into a bathroom, where she fell against a solid and unforgiving marble sink. The door was locked, and she looked for any means of escape. Finding none, she cried for a time, then eventually pulled herself up off the floor. She tore the head covering off, revealing rope burns around her neck in the mirror. She felt the burns and her tears stung her skin even more. She couldn't stand to even look at her own reflection knowing her parents would be horrified by what had become of her. She tore herself away from the image and then drank as much cold water as she could from the faucet, cupping her hands under the wet stream again and again; she had no idea when she might be able to drink clean, fresh water again. Lucy wasn't sure what they expected her to do. Shower? Whatever might happen next, she didn't want to make it easy for remotely pleasant for the men.

She combed through her long hair with her fingers, braided it tight, and tied it off with a small length of fabric she had torn from the head covering. Then she had an idea as her defiance dared to build; she tore open drawers looking for anything she might defend herself with.

The marble finish left little to pull away and use as a weapon. She tried, unsuccessfully, to pull off part of the doorframe for a wedge of wood to use as a spike. The hairdryer had already been ripped from the wall. She tried kicking at the mirror, in hopes of a glass shard to fight with. She knew she might die, but she wasn't willing to give up without a fight.

Coming up short, and with her fingers bleeding from the effort of trying to find a weapon, Lucy knew time was up as she heard someone come into the outer room. She sat on the marble floor in near defeat. Looking up in despair, she spied the shower curtain hooks. She barely had enough time to get one of them off before she heard someone opening the door. She bent open the wire, metal beads scattered the flooring, and wove the metal hook through the nape of her hair to conceal it. She hoped she might have a moment to use the makeshift weapon before her death.

The door opened. She'd learned already to not look them in the eye, but to bow to them in a subservient fashion. She would do this to stay alive for the moment.

A hand grabbed her roughly through the open door and shoved her toward the bed. She never got a chance to look at her assailant before he plunged her face down into the mattress.

The man held her with the weight of his body while he ripped the black robing from her with enough force to cut her pale skin. She suffocated under his weight as he held her down and shoved her into the mattress. Her arms flailed helplessly as she clawed to distance herself from the attacker. She screamed and fought against him, trying to crawl forward or away from him. His hands jerked her and held her down with even more force than before, causing her to lose all the breath left in her lungs. With barely enough air to scream, she turned her head to the side. She reached for the nape of her neck, groping for the metal piece—anything to fight with.

She felt his hands on her thighs. At the same time, she spied a pistol next to the bed, barely within reach. With his attention focused on trying to maneuver her legs, she took a chance. To her surprise, she frantically touched the pistol with the tips of her fingers, sliding it close enough to grasp; the cold metal felt heavy in her hands.

The man must have sensed her swift action, because his hands left her body. As she felt his weight shift, she twisted herself at the waist and fumbled while pulling back the hammer. The man barely had time to register the danger before him when she aimed blindly and fired. There was a flash, and then his heavy weight dropped onto her legs. She screamed out, not knowing yet if she'd stopped him. As the air left his lungs, she felt a wetness cover her legs. She held the gun in her hands, trembling, but he didn't move. She braced her hands into the mattress and climbed to the head of the bed, pulling her legs out from underneath him. Blood covered her. She scrambled as far away from him as possible. Terrified, she watched him and saw no rise of his chest. She heard more screaming, chanting, and more gunfire outside. She looked through the peephole in the door. After someone passed the hotel room door, she scanned the room for something to wear. She ran for the burka, threw it over her body, and covered her head.

Lucy shook, but held the gun as she opened the door a crack and looked up and down the hallway. Through the eye slits she could see that the hall was clear. Amid screams coming from several parts of the hotel, she could also hear a wicked celebration taking place somewhere. With the hallway clear, she took a chance, opening the door and running. A sign read EXIT at the end of the hall. She opened it and scrambled into the cold stairwell, ran down the concrete steps, and flew through the hotel exit.

The cold night air shocked her. As Lucy scanned the parking lot, her eyes followed the sounds of yelling and chanting. In the near distance she could make out the shadowy figures of people gathered around a big bonfire. They were caught up in their reveling and shouting, which increased when some of the figures pointed their rifles in the air and fired. Knowing this momentary distraction might be her only chance, she bolted for the dark forest beyond the parking lot. She continued to run once she'd reached the cover of the trees. She didn't look back.

~ ~ ~

By the time Lucy had finished telling her story she was hyperventilating on her own sobs. Clarisse clasped her shoulders gently. "Take a slow deep breath, Lucy; you're safe now. No one will hurt you here. You don't have to tell me more if you don't want to, but it might help you to confide in me. No one will blame you for what you did. You had every right. I would have done the same, Lucy . . . I would have done the same." Clarisse lowered her voice, and even though she didn't mean for the ill-omened tone, it came out that way. "I would have *slaughtered* him, Lucy."

Lucy whispered the admission. "I did." She was flashing back to that moment; Clarisse had seen this before with PTSD patients. Lucy sobbed openly, and Clarisse let her cry.

"There was so . . . much . . . blood. I don't remember what happened right after that. One minute I was standing there hearing gunfire and yelling; the next thing I knew, I was running through the woods with the black robe and head covering over me, and I ran into Dutch. I thought he was one of them at first, but he pulled me away from them and I went with him; as long as we were leaving there, I was fine. I killed that man," she said, and Clarisse could see the conflict in Lucy's green eyes.

"Good! He wasn't a man, Lucy. No man would ever treat you that way. His kind are less than animals," Clarisse said, holding her hands. "You survived, Lucy! That's what's important." She embraced the girl; she was proud of her. Lucy had fought back and, unlike too many other women in her situation, she had won. Now she just needed someone to help her understand that what she had done to survive was her right as a human being.

"Lucy, you are stronger than you know. You're a survivor, and I'll help you get through this. You're not alone anymore, my dear."

Clarisse had one more question for her. She held Lucy at arm's length, looked her in the eyes, and said, "I have to ask you this; was Dutch a perfect gentleman after he ran into you?"

Lucy laughed and wiped away her tears. "Dutch is like . . . a brother . . . or an uncle to me." She shook her head. "He's annoying, but yes, he was a perfect gentleman. He never touched me, but I think he knew what had happened by the way I was dressed and all the blood. He brought me hot water and clothes, but never asked me anything about it. He only wants to go north and start over. I'll miss him, but he's a loner . . . or *thinks* he's a loner; I'm not so sure."

"I know the type," Clarisse said.

After that, she examined Lucy and, though two weeks had passed since her escape, her pale, freckled skin was still covered in bruises, cuts, and scabbed-over sores. Had the assault progressed to a rape, Clarisse would have prescribed medication to expel any forming fetus. Lucy was fortunate to have saved herself from that as well; becoming impregnated by her attacker was one more problem Clarisse didn't want this girl to have to contend with.

After giving her a tetanus shot, she asked, "Lucy, may I take some blood? I'm assuming you're a carrier, but I'd like to confirm my assumption. The virus is still a danger for anyone new that we meet."

"Sure," Lucy said.

When the examination was over, Clarisse tucked Lucy safely into the clean cot next to her where Addy often slept. They'd work on her permanent living arrangement later. Beyond that, it would be a day-by-day process to build her confidence and get her over the feeling of living in a nightmare—as much as was possible in this world.

Unfortunately Clarisse had felt, more than seen, a new and foreboding coming from Dalton earlier; she knew something more terrible was at stake. If she had to guess, it had more to do than just Lucy's captors, and that brought a chill to every fiber of her being. She knew Dalton and what he was capable of.

"I'm sure he'll show up tomorrow, Bang," McCann said as he reached for the boy, still astride the mount.

"He's never done this before," Bang said. McCann could hear the sleepiness in his voice.

"Don't worry, he'll show up by morning."

After they put Mosey away for the night, they entered the cabin to find dinner held for them and Graham waiting.

"Didn't find him?" Graham asked.

"No. Heard a few wolves, but no sign of Sheriff."

Bang walked headlong into Graham, and he knew it was the boy's way of needing a hug without actually asking.

"It's all right, Bang. McCann's right, he'll show up in the morning."

McCann watched as Graham slung the boy over his shoulder and carried him into the bunkroom. *There's an unbreakable bond between those two,* McCann thought, again realizing how much he admired the man.

McCann was starving after such a long day, and after he'd eaten the stew set out for him he went in search of more leftovers. Usually Tala left a few extra biscuits out, but he was guessing that, with all the excitement today, she hadn't had the time. As he rummaged for more food, McCann peered inside the oven. Usually it held a hidden morsel or two and, luckily, there was newly dried venison jerky laid out on a cookie sheet.

"Ha!" he whispered in triumph at his discovery. After stealing a chunk, he heard someone behind him clear her throat. *Crap!* He turned to find Macy smirking at him. She was barefoot and in her nightclothes, her blond hair spilling down her neck. He swallowed and drank in the sight of her. After a moment, he cleared his own throat and said, "Hey, I'm starving. I was out looking for your dog, you know."

"No sign of him?" she asked.

"Not one," he said and leaned his hip against the counter as he looked at her. He wondered why she lingered there, leaning in the doorway. It wasn't like her to spend time alone with him without a purpose. In fact, she had always avoided being alone with him. He wondered what might be on her mind, but he'd learned to let her have her time; she'd break the silence on her own after a while—no need to rush her, let her come to him.

Macy stared at the kitchen floor, then finally said, "I can't sleep without him." She moved her blue eyes up from McCann's boots to his own brown eyes, staring back at her.

He broke the eye contact and scratched the back of his neck. He'd never been more jealous of a dog. *Hell, I'd offer to sleep at the end of her bed, but there's no way in hell I could do that and stay sane.* "Um, what can I do, Macy?"

She stood in silence staring straight at him. There was something behind those eyes. Something he wanted her to reveal to him more than anything, especially if she needed him to listen to her thoughts and feelings.

"I don't know," she said, shaking her head. Then she stopped and locked eyes with his.

A silent moment passed. "Come here," he whispered. He wasn't sure why he said it. It was more of a test for her, to find out what she was after . . . if she even knew herself. She seemed vulnerable, and this wasn't Macy—not at all.

She moved one bare foot toward him, then stopped and looked down; the trance was broken as her trusting guard took its place again. She'd come to her senses. He took a deep breath, letting it out, slow and steady, shaming himself. She was gorgeous, and he secretly loved her already, but she was still only sixteen and he was twenty.

She wasn't ready. He wanted her to come to him when the time was right. For now he would wait until she was at least eighteen. McCann took two long boot steps toward Macy and scooped her off the floor and into his arms. She didn't resist. He did not try to push away the pleasure in how soft and pliable her thighs felt resting against his arms. He carried Macy into the bunkroom, laid her down on her bed, and covered her up to her chin with her wool blanket. "Go to sleep, Macy," he whispered. "I'll sleep in the living room. If Sheriff comes back, I'll let him in." His hands were shaking as he caressed her soft cheek with the back of his hand.

McCann strolled back into the living room and collapsed on the couch after pulling off his boots and shirt. He was happy to sleep in the living room.

~ ~ ~

The next thing he knew, someone was pounding on the cabin's front door, and fresh early dawn seeped through the windows. McCann sat up and grabbed his rifle out of habit on his way to the door. After a quick glance, he sat the rifle down once he saw Dalton standing on the other side, waiting for entry at too early an hour, despite the sun's rays.

"What's up? Why so early?" McCann asked, squinting. He had a different relationship with Dalton. He liked the man, but his alliance was with Graham and even though the two men were friends, McCann wanted to preserve a distance from Dalton, not being sure that the man always had Graham's camp's best interests at heart. Something told him to keep this distance in the way his father had always taught him to treat a good neighbor: *Treat them kindly, be there if they need you, but don't go overboard or man tends to take advantage of generosity over time, breaking the best of bonds.*

He stood there in his jeans, shirtless, and with a bedhead when, suddenly Sheriff appeared on the porch and squirmed past Dalton's legs and into the cabin.

"Where the hell have you been?" McCann said to the dog. He wasn't surprised when Sheriff shot him a sideways look as if saying, *None of your business, jerk,* on his way to the bunkroom to—no doubt—find Macy.

McCann looked up at Dalton with a grim, incredulous shake of his head, and muttering things he hoped Dalton could only guess at.

"You want to talk to Graham?" McCann asked, finally opening the door to let Dalton in. Without waiting for an answer, McCann grabbed his shirt off the couch and went to wake Graham. It wasn't normal for any of them to sleep past dawn, but the previous day had been a hard one.

McCann playfully growled at Sheriff on the end of Macy's bed as he passed him on his way to Graham's room. The door was usually cracked open an inch or two, and McCann pushed it open a little and whispered Graham's name, only to find him sitting up in the darkened room, putting on his jeans. Graham nodded to him, and McCann closed the door. Still not fully awake, he returned to the kitchen as if on autopilot to start a pot of coffee.

"You guys had a long night?" Dalton asked.

"Yeah," McCann yawned. "Bang and I were out late—looking for *Sheriff.*" He said it with an emphasis on the dog's name, hoping to wake him with a little vengeance. "We didn't find him," he said as he measured the grounds into the pot.

"I know he took off after the other dogs, and Dutch hasn't found them either," Dalton said.

"Yeah, well, Macy had a hard time sleeping last night because she was worried about him. So, you're here to talk about Dutch's news?"

"Yeah, you should sit with us, too." Dalton said.

"I intend to. That girl get looked at?" McCann asked, making conversation while he took out a few coffee cups.

"Yes. Clarisse took care of her. She was at the mess tent for dinner, and I know Clarisse had her bunk with her, so she's in good hands."

"That's great. She looked pretty scared on our way to camp, but I didn't press her for conversation," McCann said.

"She's been through some things, and she actually might be able to give us some information, but I think we'll wait until Clarisse says she's ready to talk."

McCann guessed the minute he saw her that she'd been through some trauma. They'd all been through hell, but this lady had the look of shell shock.

"Good morning," Graham said from the doorway. "Coffee ready yet?"

"Not quite," McCann said as Dalton sat down at the table.

"I'm going to try and have a better day today," Graham said, lightly touching his new stitches. "At the very least, I intend to avoid the wrong end of shotguns for a while."

"Yeah, you and Rick both," Dalton said. "Steven picked out pellets for a while. Said Rick whined and milked the wound as an excuse to have more than one beer at noon."

McCann wanted them to get through this bit of cursory conversation and get down to business. He suspected Dalton was about to drop a bomb, and he wanted him to get to the point, but he remained patient as he tended to the coffee.

"We need to form a small group and go south to scout out where these invaders are," Dalton began.

"So you believe him," Graham guessed.

"Yeah, I do. He knows too much and has answers to all the right questions," Dalton said.

"How many are going?" McCann asked. He wanted to get to the point. He got that they needed to see where they were with their own eyes.

"Four, maybe five. Graham, I'd like you come, but I understand if you don't want to leave Tala right now, and your injury might slow you down. In that case, I'll take McCann here—if you're willing, that is." Dalton glanced at McCann, who nodded in response. "It's a scouting mission. We'll get in, see what we can, and then reassess the danger to us when we get back. We leave in the morning," Dalton said.

"I want to go, but you're right, I might slow you guys down," Graham said. "This concerns us all. He's certain they're Islamic terrorists?"

McCann brought three cups of coffee to the table, and Dalton took a sip. "He's positive, but that's why we're going—to make doubly sure."

"They really did this? They created mass genocide with a virus just so they could have our land?" McCann asked, shaking his head in disbelief that people could actually be so evil.

"What man does in the name of religion—or their perverted interpretation of it—has been going on for centuries, McCann," Graham tried to explain. "They're barbaric, and this is their jihad. It's what they promised."

"We're taking Steven and Sam, too. We leave at first light," Dalton said. He shot down the rest of his coffee and rose from the table.

"Is Dutch going to stick around for a few days?" Graham asked.

"I don't know. He seemed rather excited to leave," Dalton said. We'll see; the guy seems to have his own way of doing things."

McCann nodded.

"We'll be by in the morning, kid. Be ready," Dalton reminded him as he strolled out of the cabin.

"Well," Graham said as he stared out the window in contemplation. "I've never been a violent man, but if this is true, if they are responsible for this, you better believe I will be. That's what this has taught me: you must fight, or risk losing not only your life and others' but freedom itself."

"It's just hard to wrap your mind around it all," McCann admitted. "Why? Why would anyone do this?"

"I don't know, McCann, but they've tread on the wrong soil."

In the quarantine building, Dalton approached Clarisse from behind; knowing they were alone, he embraced her. She responded and turned around to face him. He kissed her. "I've missed you," he said holding her.

"We've both been busy," Clarisse admitted.

He purposely did this first, knowing he wouldn't get a chance after he broached the subject. "Clarisse, I need to talk to Lucy. She's the only one who's lived to give us information she may not even know she has," Dalton pleaded.

Clarisse stepped away from him. "Fine, Dalton, but she is very fragile right now. She nearly killed a man because she's still flashing back, and . . ."

"We're all going to be fragile or dead soon if we don't get an edge on whatever information's available to us," Dalton interrupted, raising his voice at her. He knew it was a mistake; Clarisse didn't do intimidation.

She pointed to the door but wouldn't look at him again. "*Go.* I'll bring her to you in half an hour."

"Clarisse, I'm sor—"

"Out!"

Dalton left the quarantine building knowing he couldn't say more. As he walked back, he heard the rumble of Dutch's army truck rolling into camp. He was either on his way in or out of town.

Dalton picked up his pace and walked into the clearing, where Dutch stepped out of his truck, looking around after the guards let him through the gates.

"Hey, Dutch," Rick said, extending his hand in greeting.

Dalton saw that Rick was at least vertical this morning and back to his normal self, even though he sported a leg bandage. Rick was pissed when he learned he wasn't going on the scouting mission with them, but the injury would just slow them down. Plus, they still needed him for communications.

"Hey, Dutch," said Dalton. Not worried about niceties, he continued, "You heading out? Can I convince you to stay a few days till we get back?"

"I've thought about it, and yes, I'll stay until you guys get back. I want to make sure Lucy is getting along all right and that you guys heed my warning," Dutch said.

"We're scouting in the morning," Dalton said. You want to tag along? One last mission?"

"You're still on that? You can't just take my word for it, man?" Dutch asked.

Dalton put his hands on his hips. He stared at the ground, thought about the consequences, and then looked squarely at Dutch. "No. I don't intend to just let them take our country. I'm not going to let them just have it. If it *is* them, and this is it, I'll send them all to hell or die trying. I don't know how I'm going to do that yet, but I need to make sure, and I could use your help."

He watched Dutch mull over the invitation. The cool spring air held a nip, but the sun shone in bright beams and Dalton thought it shouldn't be that way. It should be gray and misty, the kind of fog you could get lost in. Dutch's dark brown hair ran a little long. He was the same height as Dalton, but had a more muscular build, which Dalton guessed was due to farm work. He was the kind of vet who you knew, from the look in his eyes, had seen some grizzly times but had accepted that as his job to bear. Dutch was the kind you never worried about, the kind who watched your back, and Dalton hoped he'd stay with them for the battle.

"I hear you," Dutch said, and nothing more was needed to make him understand the way Dalton felt. "When I first came across your message, I thought you guys were just a bunch of lucky civilians who just happen to have an old HAM operator playing on the waves. I didn't know you were a tiny army." He took a deep breath and faced the sun's rays for a second before looking back at Dalton. "Hell, if you're willing to take the risk, I'll tag along. I'll do it for Lucy, and the last infidels."

Dalton chuckled at the reference. "That's what we are, aren't we? The last infidels. Those bastards . . ." He picked up the seriousness of his gesture and tipped his head at Dutch. "Sounds fine to me. Glad you're with us." Dalton shook the man's hand again, this time with brotherly respect.

"For now I'd like to check in on Lucy and then I need to find my damn dogs," Dutch said.

"They're still missing?" Dalton asked.

"Yep. They're well trained; this isn't like them," Dutch said.

"Well, Sheriff over at Graham's camp was out all night, but just showed up this morning. He'd never done that before either. I'm sure they'll turn up."

"Great. Well, that's the least of our problems right now," Dutch said, then asked Dalton, "We leave at sunrise?"

"You know it." Dalton looked past their gate and saw Clarisse heading in his direction with Lucy in tow. He knew Clarisse well enough to see she was still madder than hell.

"Hey, guys, Clarisse is here with Lucy."

"Hey Sport, how you getting along?" Dutch asked Lucy.

She flashed him a smile and then it was gone, but Dalton thought that was probably a great achievement for Lucy. Then he realized Clarisse was burrowing her eyes into him.

"I told Lucy you needed to question her. Where do you want to do this? I'll give you ten minutes, and I'll be present," Clarisse said.

Dalton nodded and put up both of his hands. "That's fine, Clarisse. Let's go into the communications tent. Can Sam attend? He always has a different perspective on these things."

Clarisse looked like she wanted to explode at him and sever a few important body parts; she was only barely holding it together. She blew out a frustrated breath, turned to Lucy, and held onto her arm gently.

"Lucy, it's important they get the advantage of all the details of what you witnessed. You'll have two or three people asking you questions, but I'll be there for you. Can you do this for us?" Clarisse asked.

"I'll be there too, Lucy," Dutch said in his low raspy voice.

Dalton knew he cared for the girl more than he let on. She looked terrified to Dalton, and ready to flee. He wouldn't blame her if she did.

Lucy looked at him with her light-green eyes; her lips trembled. Dalton was about to call it off when she nodded her quivering chin and tears spilled over and ran down her cheeks.

He reached to comfort her, but Clarisse and intervened. He should have known it was stupid to try. He needed to be careful with her, but *damn the animals that did this to her*.

Clarisse hugged her briefly and then turned her toward the communications tent. Dalton and the others followed, but before they entered, Clarisse turned to face them with a glare.

"I'm warning you, go easy," she said as she guided Lucy inside the tent and left the rest to ponder her warning. "She always like this?" Dutch asked.

"Clarisse? No. Actually, she can be your best friend. Or your worst nightmare; seems I've crossed the line here lately," Dalton admitted.

"My kind of lady," Dutch said as he passed Dalton into the tent.

"Great," Dalton mumbled as he waited for Sam to join them.

"Do you have everything?" Tala asked McCann.

"Yes, ma'am," he said as he pulled the strings taut on his pack.

"What about your med kit?" Marcy asked him.

"Got it."

"McCann, you got the extra magazine?" Graham called from the dining room.

"Sure do," he exclaimed. Their questions were starting to drive him a little crazy. "You guys, I need to travel light. I'll probably be back by tomorrow night or the next morning. Don't worry."

"Plan for the worst, hope for the best," Graham said, remembering what his father always used to say.

"Yeah, *my* dad said that, too."

"Where are you going?" Bang asked. He'd come in the door without making a sound and, though they weren't hiding the fact that McCann was going on a dangerous scouting mission with the preppers, they hadn't told him or the rest of the group yet.

McCann looked at Tala, and Tala looked at Graham as if someone else might have the answer.

"He's leaving in the morning to go with the preppers on a scouting trip. He should be back in a day or two. We're trying to make sure he has all the stuff he might need," Graham said.

"When were you going to tell me?" Macy said from the doorway, not yet visible to the others. Everyone looked from Macy to McCann.

"Macy, it's not a big deal. I thought you heard about it this morning," McCann explained.

"Why can't I go too?" she asked.

"Macy," Graham answered before anyone else could, "this isn't one of those times where you're being kept out because you're a girl; he's going because I can't go."

"Okay. Still, why can't I go, too?" she asked.

"There isn't room in the Jeep for more than five, Macy, and I need you here to take care of the horses. You're the only one they're not too skittish around," McCann said.

Mark was about to protest that assessment when McCann widened his eyes at him to get him to clam up.

"Yeah," Mark shook his head. "Mosey kicked me last time I mucked out the stalls," he said, staring at the floor.

"That's because Macy talks to them when she's in there alone. I've heard her," Bang said.

"I do not!" Macy said, leaving the room.

McCann let out a frustrated breath and thought it was getting a little too stuffy in the cabin. They were seldom all indoors during the day at the same time anymore since the weather had warmed up. Even Sheriff was still lollygagging on the wood floor of the bunkroom, sleeping off his adventures of the night before.

McCann would miss them all, but it was a just a little trip. But it also happened to be the longest trip he'd be taking since he rode into town, and potentially more dangerous than he could fathom. No story ever foretold such calamities so close to home. No one ever predicted this kind of hell. It was one thing to imagine independence as a teenager, to long for it even, but it was something else to survive everyone you ever knew and be expected to go on day after day. Just when McCann thought that might even be possible, the story had now changed.

Now not only had there been a massive pandemic that had wiped out humankind, but someone had done it on purpose and that someone was now here on their own land, in America, and boasting about it, proud of it.

"You know, McCann . . ." Graham said, interrupting McCann's thoughts and causing him to look up from packing. He noticed that everyone was gone except Graham.

"When I taught math at the University of Washington, my attitude about war and fighting was very different from how it is now; life has a way of teaching you out of your best intentions. I didn't believe in patriotism; I only believed in humanity, and that we should embrace our enemies. The only problem with that way of thinking is that, while you're embracing your enemies, they're flying our own planes into buildings, killing thousands of innocent people. They're developing evil plans to corrupt a religion and declare jihad on anyone who denounces them." He pounded his cane out of frustration to the floor. "Dammit, I was wrong. It wasn't us; it was them. They were plotting genocide while I was trying to embrace them. Everything I tried to stand for, every argument I won, was nothing more than blind faith in humanity where evil will remain a component.

"I once was blind, McCann. Now I see, and if there is any way we can stop them, we will. You come back to us in one piece. We're going to need you." He reached out for a handshake and then pulled McCann in.

"Will do, Graham." McCann was thankful for Graham's concern, but then added, in a worried voice, "Make damn sure Macy doesn't follow us."

Graham looked serious. "I'll tie her up somewhere."

"Good luck with that," McCann said jokingly, though in fact he was completely serious.

Lucy sat down in a metal folding chair inside the media tent, amid a hum of electronics. Her pale slender hands were like icicles, and she pushed them down between her thighs for warmth. Clarisse had given her fatigues and a pair of hiking boots to wear. She was thankful to finally wear clothing that actually fit her instead of having to adjust Dutch's much-too-large apparel. They weren't fashionable by any means, but at least they were hers, and now she felt more secure.

Sam pointed a space heater toward her to warm up her legs. She'd met him the night before at dinner along with several other people. She also met with Rick and cried when she apologized to him, fearing he would be angry with her. He wasn't, of course, but she knew he didn't trust her either.

"Lucy," Clarisse said, "tell us what you remember. Just start from the beginning and know that we might stop you briefly to ask you questions along the way. Please just answer the best you can. We can stop anytime you need to. This is a safe place, and we are your friends. No one is going to harm you here."

"Okay. I . . . lived near Spokane in a little town called Liberty Lake." She looked up and saw several people nod, acknowledging that they knew where the place was; the town was the last stop in Washington along Interstate 90 before the Idaho border.

She shook her head. "I thought I was the only one left there. It's really just a big suburban neighborhood. I lived with my parents in a house on Settler Road and worked at the Safeway grocery store there right in the middle of town. I was going to school at Eastern Washington University, and when the virus broke out, they shut the school down." She stared into her lap. "My parents . . . they died. My little brothers, too." Her tears fell to her lap, making darker pooling stains of green on the camo fabric of her pants. Clarisse handed her a

125

clean cloth, and Sam wrapped a wool army blanket around her shoulders.

Lucy swallowed and smiled once she blotted the tears away. "It all happened so fast. At first the city council coordinated burials of the dead in Pavilion Park, near where I lived. Then, a few weeks later, there were just too many, and my father told me to keep inside and to lock the doors. To pretend we weren't home or that all of us were dead. I never got sick. I never came down with the virus; I just watched as my mother and brothers passed. My dad and I buried them all in the backyard. Then my father came down with it, and I sat with him when he died. I was alone then; winter came, and I buried my father. It was cold and the ground was hard; it took me two days to do it. I survived by rationing what food I could get from the neighbors' empty houses and whatever canned food was left at the grocery stores. He wanted me to kill myself," she said, breaking into more tears. "He didn't want me to be alone, but I couldn't do it. I couldn't . . ." she looked to them for approval.

Dalton leaned forward, but again Clarisse pulled him back. "I'm okay," Lucy said. She wiped away more tears and took a deep breath.

"I did what he said; I stayed inside and pretended that there was no one home. At first, there were sounds like raiders searching homes, and I was terrified someone would break in and discover me, and then there were no sounds at all. You could always hear the highway from our home late at night when you went to sleep. I grew up with that sound as a young girl. But now it was silent. Too quiet; I couldn't sleep. There were no cars going anywhere, no neighbors shouting or kids playing basketball on the road out front. Nothing.

I had enough food. My dad had made sure I would, but I just couldn't stand it anymore. I waited for it to get dark, and at first I walked down to the end of our road. I went and checked the mail, thinking that maybe someone might still deliver it and . . . I don't know why I did it." She looked confused, shaking her head and questioning her own logic.

"I kept doing it each evening, checking the empty mailbox and walking to the end of the street just to see . . . something . . . anything or anyone. Then winter came again, and the snow kept me inside because I didn't want to have my footprints showing; my dad had warned me about that. So, I played my piano during the day quietly, worked out in the afternoon, and read a lot. I kept myself on a schedule to keep from going crazy. Our power was out, but the gas fireplace still worked, so I stayed warm enough.

"Finally the snow melted and no more came. I was out of books to read and thought if I could only break into the library, I might be able to keep from going insane. It was the farthest I'd ventured from home since my father passed away. Only about half a mile. When I got there, I saw that someone had already torn it to shreds." She shook her head, trying to fathom the unfathomable. "I don't know who would do that. It scared me. So I ran, and then a dog chased me; I only barely made it back into my house and shut the door. Then more dogs came, and they growled at me. I felt trapped, and I knew I wouldn't be able to get out again. By this time I was down to a few weeks of food left. I'd planned to go to the nearby grocery store to see if I could find anything there that might be left over, but after finding the library in bad shape, I didn't think the grocery stores would be any better and the dogs might get me."

She took a deep breath. "Then one day, I thought I was dreaming because I was asleep early one morning and I heard the rumble of vehicles on the highway again. Later I heard shooting and I thought that maybe the military had come to help. Maybe other survivors I didn't know about were with them, and I was afraid I might be left behind. So I got up and took a baseball bat with me in case I needed it for the feral dogs, and I ran into town.

127

"A dog came after me, and I was trying to fight it off when I heard gunfire, and the dog dropped dead. I turned around and . . . it wasn't the military. They didn't look like any of us. They wore cloths over their face like the terrorists I've seen on TV. It was them."

"Did they speak English?" Dalton asked her.

"Um, one of them did . . . kind of. The one that shot the dog grabbed me by my hair and pushed me to the ground. I tried to run, but I couldn't. He spoke some other language and yelled for someone else. He pointed his gun at me, so I stayed right where I was. Then this other guy came, and he was even meaner. He jerked me up and screamed at me in another language. He made me kneel down in front of him. Then he demanded in English to know if I could say one word in Arabic. I don't know any Arabic. He kept screaming at me and I shook my head no. He said again that if I knew one word in Arabic, I would live; if not, I would die. So, I shut my eyes and started crying. I didn't want to see him shoot me. I just hoped it would be over soon."

"Lucy, what kind of weapons were they carrying?" Sam's soft voice broke the awful tension of remembering again.

She sniffed and wiped her face. "Um, they were rifles. I don't know what they're called. They would pull the trigger and it would fire several bullets at a time. They were black. They also had knives, and one even had a whip. Some of them would point the rifles in the sky and fire them over and over while screaming, like it was some kind of celebration," she said, as though trying to make sense of it all.

Sam nodded in understanding. Then Clarisse said, "So the second man had you and asked you to speak in Arabic, then what happened?"

"Then he pulled me to my feet and tied my hands behind my back and other men clawed at me and pulled my hair as he dragged me through a crowd. Then I saw at least twenty people standing with black hoods on and they were leashed with ropes to an army truck. I couldn't believe what was happening. Some of them were crying, and then I realized they were only girls; I could tell by their voices. One of them tried to sit on the ground, and one of the other men beat her with a stick over and over until she stood up. The guy who had me was waiting for someone else. He stood there talking to someone. I couldn't understand what he was staying. I said to him, 'Please let me go.' And he pushed me to the ground and kicked me, then pulled me back up. Finally, another man came and I think he was the boss. He took out a knife. It was curved . . . about twelve inches long . . . and he held it to my neck. He asked me again if I knew even one word in Arabic, but I didn't. Then . . ." she looked up at them.

"It's okay, Lucy. Just say it," Clarisse encouraged her. "There is nothing these men haven't seen the brutality of. It's okay."

"He asked me if I was a—a virgin." She cried at the humiliation. "By then, I knew who they were. I said I wasn't. I knew then that he would kill me, and the only thing I could think as the time slowed was that I'd rather be shot than have my throat slit. Is that—selfish?"

"No, Lucy, that's human," Dutch said.

Tears streamed down Lucy's cheeks and she nodded her head, as if the riddle to that dilemma had passed. It was okay to fear death, in any way it might be delivered.

"How many men do you think there were, Lucy?" Dalton asked.

She shook her head. "I don't know. From what I could see at that time, there were at least twenty trucks all lined up going east toward Idaho. There were several parked on the main street, but mostly I could see several more on the highway from the main street. I want to say I saw at least three hundred men, but there could have been many more than that. I just don't know, because after that he pulled me up to him like he was deciding something. He grabbed my hair and then shoved me back at the second guy and said something

129

in Arabic. That guy pulled a black robe over me and then put a black hood over my head. He then tied me up with the other girls. We were there for another hour. I tried to see through my hood, but the guard would beat us if we moved. We didn't dare talk to one another. The others cried; many sounded even younger than me." She shook her head in sorrow.

"Then they were shouting, and all of a sudden, truck engines started, and the one I was tied to began to move. We were pulled and made to walk behind it. Every now and then I got a glimpse of where we were going. We went back to the highway and, in the right lane, trucks went much slower with prisoners tied to the back, walking, while in the other lane army trucks went much faster, flying by us. Some of the girls would push toward the outer lane and someone with a whip would cut us across the legs to stay to the right."

"Did you ever get to speak to any of the other prisoners?" Dalton asked.

"No," she said.

"Did you hear their voices at all? Did they sound American, or did you detect any other accent?"

"No, there was nothing but the wailing of young girls. I swear they were no more than fifteen," Lucy said, shaking her head.

"Okay, how long ago was this? Do you remember?" Sam asked.

"Two to three weeks ago," she said.

"This might sound like a strange question," Sam interjected, "but did the robe and hood smell like? Did it have an odor?"

"It smelled like sweat and iron. It was damp and dirty."

"So, other than them questioning you, you didn't hear any English?" Dalton asked.

"No, not then."

"Okay, Lucy, keep going. You're almost there," Clarisse said, and Dalton suddenly didn't want to hear anymore. He wanted her to stop there because he could guess what happened next. He'd seen the aftermath, what these animals had done, but he needed to find out how she got away. That was the mystery to him.

After another deep breath, Lucy continued. "So we stopped, near Post Falls, Idaho. I kept tripping and almost fell over. I was so thankful when we stopped. It was night, and some of the girls started weeping even more, like they knew what was next. I didn't, but I was really scared. I heard someone come for one of the girls, she fought whoever was trying to take her, and then he beat her. She finally screamed, 'Kill me!' Then there was a gunshot. Those were the only words of English I heard spoken by the others: *Kill me*.

"I huddled in my spot. I didn't look, I didn't know what would happen. Then someone pulled off my hood and then pulled it back on, as if checking to see which one I was. He untied me from the rope line and I caught a glance of a hotel with rooms from the outside. I remembered seeing this place, years ago, when we'd pass by it on the highway. That's how I knew we were near Post Falls. He shoved me through a door and then into the bathroom of the room and locked me in there. He said something in Arabic that I didn't understand.

"I took off the hood. I washed my hands. I braided my hair and looked around for a weapon, anything I could fight back with. I drank a lot of water from the faucet. There was no window to escape from. Then, I heard someone at the door. I'd looped a shower curtain hook into my hair, hoping to use it to fight with if I could. But I didn't get that chance. The door opened and the man who liked my hair shoved me into the main room." She looked at Clarisse, and her voice could no longer form the words.

"Did he tell you his name, Lucy?" Dutch asked her, hoping to speed her past the worst part.

She shook her head, because she couldn't speak with the lump in her throat.

"Was he their leader?" Sam asked.

"I don't know. I think he might have been, since the others seemed to look to him for answers."

Dalton took in a breath. "Lucy, did he rape you?"

"No," she answered, her eyes wide with tears streaming down her cheeks. "I shot him before he could"

It wasn't what Dalton expected to hear. She'd somehow gotten away. He drew a hand down his face and sighed in relief. "Thank God, Lucy. You're a fighter. Good girl! How did you get away?" Dalton asked.

"I don't really know; it happened so fast. He was trying to hurt me, and I fought him and saw his gun on the nightstand. I grabbed it and took a chance. There were gunshots in the distance, like before, and singing. People chanting crazy things . . . my hands shook. I was so scared. I couldn't stop. I thought I'd mess it up, but it went off. I killed him. I shot him in the chest and killed him. There was blood everywhere. He fell on me and I pulled myself out from under him. There was more gunfire outside. I threw the burka and hood back on, opened the door and . . . I don't know. I was so scared. I ran. I barely remember what happened between the time I left and when I woke up the next morning at Dutch's place."

"Did you have shoes on?" Sam asked.

"I never took my tennis shoes off; they were still on."

"What did you do with the gun, Lucy?" Dalton asked.

"I don't know. I don't remember."

"You didn't bring it with you?" Sam asked.

"No. I must have dropped it."

"How'd you get past the others without them seeing you?" Sam asked.

"I don't know. I opened the door, crouched down, and kept to the railing. There was a bonfire in the parking lot. With all the yelling and shouting, they weren't watching. I got lucky, I guess. I don't know."

"So, that's when you ran into Dutch?" Dalton asked.

"Yes, afterward, when I was running through the woods; I ran behind the hotel complex and just kept going. I barely remember—I kept seeing his bloody face in my mind—I ran into someone and I thought they'd caught me, and that was it. Except he pulled me farther away, and that was the direction I wanted to go, anyway, so I didn't fight him."

"Dutch, this sound about right?" Dalton asked.

"Yeah. I pulled the hood off her and saw she was a local in the wrong getup. She was covered in blood, man. I guessed what had taken place. She's right. I heard them carrying on. Couldn't believe this was on my own soil. Every now and then, you heard them scream, 'Bismillah al-rahman al-rahim'—in the name of God, the most gracious, the most merciful—and shoot off like the demon misfits they are. Like I said before, this is a mop-up exercise. We are the last infidels. The last unbelievers."

Dalton noticed how Clarisse visibly shook. He touched her back, trying to calm her. She let him. They were all afraid. Hell, he was scared shitless himself, but he'd kill every last one of them given the chance.

Lucy looked at Dutch and asked quietly, "You knew?"

He filled his lungs with air. "Yes. I've seen it before. I'm sure a few of us have. This is their M.O. They have no regard for women. They're nothing more than animals. You passed out shortly after I got you. It wasn't a stretch and I figured, if you needed to, you'd tell me in your own time when you were ready. It didn't matter. I got you away from there the next day. If I'd babied you, you wouldn't have been able to function, Lucy."

"I understand. Thank you for taking care of me, Dutch."

"No problem, kid."

"Okay, anyone else have questions?" Clarisse asked, but no one volunteered another.

"Thank you, Lucy," Dalton said. "You've helped us more than you know."

McCann heard the engine before it even traversed their long driveway. They were all attuned to the minutest of sounds; even a deer entering the cabin's clearing in moonlight, pulling at the dewy grass, registered in their subconscious, or the first busy bees of spring flying like overburdened dump trucks into the glass windowpanes. It was amazing to him, the sounds of nature that he'd never paid attention to before.

He'd thought about waking the others to say good-bye, but he didn't want his departure to be a big deal. Not as he was going off into danger.

He padded into the living room with his gear held aloft. He stopped at the door and glanced at Macy's bunk. He nodded his head at Sheriff as if telling the dog to be on watch over her now.

"Leaving without saying good-bye?" Graham said in the darkness of the living room, scaring the living daylights out of McCann. Graham had waited for him there, he realized.

"I don't want a long, sappy farewell. I'll be back in a few days," McCann said.

Graham nodded hid understanding. While McCann put on his boots, Graham couldn't help but give another warning. "You may see things, McCann, that will burn into your mind. Inhuman images you can't rid yourself of. I want you to know life is worth living in any possible form. Don't ever give it up."

"I don't plan on getting myself captured, Graham. I'll be back in a few days." The headlights of the Jeep flashed twice into the window, signaling McCann to hurry up.

"I've got to go," he said.

"Take care, McCann." Graham embraced the young man and slapped him on the back before opening the door for him to join the others.

As McCann walked toward the headlights, he had the bitter sense that guilt overtook Graham because he couldn't make the trip himself. If something were to happen to him, Graham would be the man that needed to go on, not him. The fault would weigh on Graham's soul, and for that reason alone McCann would make sure he came back in one piece.

He turned back after loading his pack into the back and waved. With the lights shining past his form and blotting out all of his features, Graham could only saw his shadow outlined, but he waved back.

McCann slid into his seat next to Sam. Dalton, in the driver's seat, said, "Ready?" McCann nodded, and they backed out of the driveway and down the long, cold road. No one said a thing for miles. He stared out the window at a dark landscape of hope.

I will come back to them. I will return, he kept telling himself. *I have to. They can't do it without me.* He continued to tell himself this as they rumbled on for miles over the gravelly, unkempt roads.

"You know, we ought to use some of this debris to make several blockades over roadways where they can't easily get around," Sam said.

"I have some experience in doing just that, in a faraway desert land," Dalton said.

"Hell, I'm sure you do," Dutch said, then added, "but we didn't have much in the way of trees and foliage to work with then; it was mostly rocks and sand . . . endless sand."

"That's an advantage we have here. They get cold there in Iraq, Iran, Afghanistan—hell, wherever they crawled out from under—but they don't have trees and coverage the way we do. That's probably why they waited for spring. They couldn't handle the temps up here over the winter," Dalton speculated.

"Damn, it gets cold at night. I remember that," Steven said and then paused. "They've probably been here for a lot longer than we thought. Florida, Texas, I bet they're just getting to us now."

They were all quiet after that statement—too quiet. McCann wasn't sure what was worse, having them talk doom and gloom or this silence. They didn't really know what they'd find, but they all suspected it would be a nightmare. They kept going, speeding down the debris-strewn roads, heading south. Occasionally they avoided some obstacle in the street, passing through ghost towns. McCann remembered how eerie it had been when he'd seen these ghost towns last winter on horseback; now it was even worse. Since then the snowpack had collapsed several roofs. Fires had broken out and burned part of one town to the ground, with only black sticks marking the graves of the buildings.

"McCann, when you came to town last winter, did you travel as the crow flies, or did you follow the roadway?" Sam asked him.

McCann thought Sam already knew the answer to the question before he asked it, but he was trying to make conversation. "It would be too hard on the horses' hooves to make a road trip that long, and it took longer than I thought it would with all the snow. I rode the crow line south. I cut several days off that way, but it was still a foolhardy trip. I should have waited, but I had to get out of Carnation. It was too quiet." A chill ran up his spine, remembering how he'd come halfway before realizing that leaving in winter was a mistake. He'd almost frozen to death as the winds whipped at him, stealing his breath, freezing his eyelids shut, and making him so sleepy he didn't care when the reaper came. It was hard now to imagine how he'd survived it. He didn't remember parts of the trip at all.

"A trip like that'll make a man out of you," Sam said.

"Yeah, I think it did," McCann agreed.

Tala sat on a soft blanket spread over the damp ground, resting in the shade of a generous pine tree. The cold damp had finally given way to warmth enough for bare arms and short sleeves to work at weeding the spring garden. They weeded daily now, but even that didn't seem often enough; spring weed sprouts threatened to strangle the life out of their precious new vegetable starts.

"Well, if you're going to sit there, you have to at least tell us stories while we work," Mark said.

Knowing he was only kidding with her, Tala said, "You got it. If that's the price to pay for a break, I'm all for it." She was full of tales told by her American Indian grandparents; she retold them because they reminded her of the old ways—the way things used to be and seemed now to be again.

Sometimes she'd recall them when she needed to remind them of a life lesson. Sometimes, they just came to her for no particular reason she could think of, stories just begging to be retold.

Tala watched as Mark, Marcy, and Bang bent and pulled at the stubborn weeds. It was a necessity that they work each day like this; it was time again for children to labor as workers, and she felt that chores really were the best way to bring children up in the world. Idleness never benefitted anyone. In the past kids had always needed and wanted to work, to help their elders, but for some reason those lessons had been lost in the now-departed modern world. She hoped they would remember this lore, these stories—now and in the future.

As she tried to think of a story, something nagged at Tala's subconscious and she took stock of her new family. Graham was safe at the prepper camp helping Rick, and she expected Clarisse to show up soon with Addy and the new one, Lucy. She wasn't sure what bothered her, and she rubbed her backside knowing she'd pushed herself too much lately with work.

She pushed away the annoyance of the unnamed thing and reached into her mind to select a story from the bevy in her memory bank. Having McCann away on the scouting trip weighed on them all, but he was a grown man and Tala knew he could look out for himself. She sensed no tragedy there to befall him, but she could be mistaken. She hoped not, for all their sakes—especially Macy's. She sighed, leaning against the tree trunk with her belly resting on her lap, looking at the others working, bent over or squatted down. Bees buzzed by them without malice on their mission. She watched as Mark's rifle slung over his back had slid down to his side and dangled from the strap, getting into his way. It was cumbersome work, weeding with a rifle, but it was a necessary precaution. Marcy passed him and silently nudged his rifle over to his backside again. Tala knew they carried a love for one another. It was something she and Graham also shared. *Those two are meant for one another*, she thought. Mark's presence in Marcy's life calmed her flighty spirit somehow.

"Did I ever tell you guys about how Bear got his claws?"

"No. I don't remember that one," Bang said, squatting down to plunge his little fingers into the earth in earnest on either side of a determined dandelion root. He used a screwdriver after he made some headway to work farther down the root, creating a free channel to help extract the thing in its entirety.

"Good. Okay, so, there once was a time when Bear lived side by side with Man, much like a tame dog does today. Only Bear also advised man and sat with him on wise councils and hunted, played music, and walked beside Man in life every day. Then one day a young warrior claimed that Bear had killed another man on a hunting trip. What had really happened was that the warrior had killed the other man so that he could claim his wife, but he blamed the murder on Bear.

"The father of the young man was the chief of the tribe, and he believed his son. The great council came together and Bear defended his kind, but it was no use. Man stood against Bear and ordered the death of the accused.

"When Man came to carry out the sentence, Bear resisted and bared his fangs at Man. Man tried to speak with reason that justice must be carried out, but Bear said, 'Your justice is of your own making. If you carry out your justice, Bear will forever hunt the evil of your kind and shall never shake Man's hand again, and instead rip you limb from limb.' Man ignored Bear's warning and carried out the wrongful death sentence. Bear then left Man's side, and from that day forward Bear grew claws and never did shake Man's hand again. Instead, Man now fears bear— especially if he's an evil Man."

Tala looked up and saw that they had all stopped what they were doing and stared at her, mouths agape. A moment passed in silence.

"You're supposed to tell *nice* stories," Bang said.

Mark and Marcy laughed.

"Oh, I'm sorry, Bang. It's just an Indian legend," Tala said, then saw movement beyond them through the wire gating surrounding the garden. Clarisse and two others walked their way.

"They're here," Tala said, bracing herself against the tree to stand up. She waved at them and, as they approached, Tala noticed how Bang moved behind Mark when he saw Addy. Tala knew this was going to be a challenge, but thought the best thing to do was let the transition happen naturally.

"Hi, you're not working too hard, are you?" Clarisse asked her.

"No, I was just taking a break and telling stories. I guess the last one was a little scary."

"I'll say," Mark said. "I'm going to have nightmares now. Man betrays Bear. Bear grows claws and kills evil men from then into eternity. Nice one!"

Marcy shoved him and giggled.

Tala huffed. "I don't know why that one came to me. It is pretty scary."

"Well, let's get to work. You guys stopped about there?" Clarisse said, pointing to the area still embedded with weeds.

Tala caught Clarisse's eye, knowing she had picked up on Bang's tension as well. They'd both agreed earlier to expose the two to one another often enough to help Bang get over his guilt and his fear of Addy.

Tala handed the newcomers their own buckets, and they all began again while Tala stood watch and offered the others water that they'd brought with them that morning.

"Are you getting along okay, Lucy?" Tala asked her to make her feel a part of the group.

"Oh, yes," Lucy smiled. "Everyone has been very nice. I'm going to be working in the kitchen now with Rick's wife Olivia and helping Clarisse out in the infirmary. I'll get to see everyone a few times a day, and I'm so thankful to be around people again. And Olivia doesn't seem to be upset with me for hurting her husband."

"We all understand, Lucy," Tala said with compassion. That comment seemed to ease Lucy's fears, and she went back to work among the others.

After another hour of occasional conversation, Tala watched as the sun rose to midday, and she called it quits. The crew packed up their buckets and tossed the weeds into the forest to rot on the pine floor. They stood back and surveyed the garden with hope. The tender young greens were thriving now; everything they'd worked for over the winter was now coming to fruition. Before they headed in, they picked enough early salad leaves and radishes for the evening meal.

"I can't wait for carrots," Marcy said in longing.

"Green beans," Mark nodded.

"No, it's the tomatoes I'm waiting for. I can smell them from here," Clarisse said.

Tala noticed Bang pull away, and she realized Addy wasn't privy to the conversation around her. She watched as Bang stopped in front of Addy and awkwardly signed the question as to which crop she most looked forward to.

She signed *strawberries* with a shy smile.

Bang agreed. Red, juicy strawberries would be the best of all.

They'd decided the night before to head west to Interstate 5. Dutch figured the invaders were sticking to the major highways and would eventually make their way inland. For now, he'd bet they'd go for securing major cities via main highways and then move inland.

This technique made sense to Dalton tactically, so their plan of action was to see just how close the invaders were to their homestead. That meant traveling west through the little towns of Concrete, Hamilton, and Lyman near Sedro Woolley, along State Highway 20. It flanked a hair north of the Skagit River until it reached Burlington, where it blossomed into little cities. There Highway 20 met Interstate 5, which ran south to Seattle and all the way to Los Angeles.

If he were the invaders, Dalton would make sure to secure the port of Bellingham and work his way down. "They're too damn close," had been his conclusion the night before when they studied the map. "It's only fifty miles away to Burlington."

"If they wanted to, they could be at our camp in little more than an hour," was Sam's response.

"Well, don't do anything to attract their attention," Rick had warned them all in jest.

"We won't," answered Dalton. "We'll go take a look and see if they're that far up and then go as far south as we need to. Hopefully we won't see any sign of them."

"You guys have an exit strategy from camp? Just in case?" Dutch had asked.

"Yeah. Pick forest service and back roads through these mountains north of us and deport into Canada," Steven said, pointing at the map.

But Dutch had disagreed. "Again, man, these guys don't recognize borders. There's no asylum up there."

"No, but there's Mount Baker, and this is our terrain. We know these mountains better than them. That's our advantage. There are still places in here no man has ever seen. We could hide our whole village for a lifetime in there; no one would ever find us," Sam had said.

"We're not leaving to give up our land if I have anything to say about it," Dalton chimed in, causing an end to the conversation. "Let's call it a night."

~ ~ ~

Thinking back on the previous night's meeting, Dutch regarded Sam; he wasn't like the rest, and Dutch was now beginning to see why they valued his input; Sam knew things, useful things. More and more, Dutch was beginning to like these people.

This morning they'd traveled slowly through the little town of Concrete. Debris was scattered over every inch, and the secondary dam that had blocked part of an inlet creek feeding into the Skagit River rushed out of control with the spring thaw, threatening the roadway. But there was nothing else to see other than how the animals had taken over, reclaiming the grounds for their own. An entire herd of deer hung out at the corner of Superior Avenue and the Cascade Loop, where a truck stop and restaurant stood. Some of the animals got up and moved out of the roadway, but others were more inclined to let Dalton maneuver around them.

"These herds are growing like crazy," Steven said.

"More territory," McCann put in.

"Yeah, now that the plague of man is gone, wildlife will fill in the gaps," Sam said.

"You think there's anything here worth stopping for?" Steven asked.

"Nah, it looks like it's been hit pretty hard, and we need to focus on the mission instead of resources this time. Let's get in, get the data, and get out," Dalton said as he steered around a random tractor tire abandoned in the middle of the road.

McCann looked around for the tractor that had lost the tire. "Don't know where the hell that came from."

"Nothing makes sense in this world anymore; don't even try," Steven advised the younger man.

"That's for sure," McCann said.

They'd just passed Lyman, and Dalton felt tension rise inside the Jeep's cabin the closer they got to their destination. There was no more idle chatter in the backseat. They were all on alert and watching for clues. Another twenty minutes and he expected to see more than merely random tires in the road, garbage strewn by Mother Nature, and forest animals foraging on the leftovers of humankind.

As they neared Burlington, more and more relics of civilization appeared. They slowed down to a crawl, weaving in and out of parked cars and remnants of storm debris mangled on the highway, but nothing yet looked like recent human activity. What remained was more a collective randomness that reminded them of the massive loss of civilization. By the time they got to where Highway 20 turned into Fairhaven Avenue and intersected South Burlington Boulevard, they stopped; the entrance was blocked completely by what appeared to be a medevac helicopter.

"Past or present?" Dalton asked after a moment of contemplation.

Sam leaned up to check around at the roadways. "Past," he said after a moment's hesitation, then leaned back into the seat.

"How do you know?" Dutch asked out of curiosity.

Sam leaned forward again and pointed. "See that? That's your pilot, or part of him. He's been picked clean and the skull's been bleached by the sun."

"How do you know he's the pilot?" Dutch asked.

"The rest of him is over there," he pointed to the other side of the road, "in the uniform. With all the debris and dirt on the road, I can see from here that there aren't any footprints. The cabin door's still open and rain rot has caused the interior dyes to leach down the white siding. Anyone could throw debris around to make it look old, but not without leaving traces. This stuff hanging from the rotor blades has stained the paint underneath. It's been there a while. There's bird shit all over, and it's dripped downward. That thing's been here since the start."

"Think there's still med equipment in there?" Steven asked.

"We're not stopping now," Dalton said.

"This place is creeping me out. We're too much in the open here," Dutch said.

Dalton put the Jeep in reverse and saw a way to turn left through a store parking lot to bypass the intersection altogether. Once they made the turn, they went another few blocks south parallel to Interstate 5 and squeezed between several cars. Dalton focused on the route in front of him. "Keep your eyes peeled for any movement," he said to the crew.

They had just approached West Fairhaven Avenue on South Burlington Boulevard; West Fairhaven led to the west through two blocks of neighborhood and disappeared under Interstate 5. There was a clear view of the highway from their vantage point before they crossed over to the other side.

"Guy, three o'clock," Sam said dryly and, for a split second, Dalton thought Sam joked. Then he remembered Sam didn't joke—ever.

He turned his head to the right just in time to see a form standing by a military Humvee on the overpass of Interstate 5 in the middle of town, pointing a rifle at them.

"*Fuuuck* me! Those bastards!" Steven said.

"Back up, back up, back up!" Dutch shouted. "Movement on the lower left. Cover!"

As soon as Dalton heard the warning, he threw the Jeep into reverse and the first few pings snipped past their location. They'd been seen, and there was nothing immediate to take cover behind. The nearest building was a towing company, and the building itself was covered in corrugated metal. A barrage of bullets cascaded onto the tin roof, emitting a noise like nothing they'd heard in a very long time, and then far away.

The abandoned helicopter remained in their escape path. Dalton swung the Jeep into drive and raced back the way they'd come, through the parking lot of the shopping center, back through town, and turned right on Spruce Street right behind an office building before he stopped.

"Was it just one guy?" Dalton asked. His heart beat out of his chest and he found himself automatically using his old tricks from his military days to calm his pulse down.

"No, there were at least three shooters," Dutch said.

"Son of a bitch!" Dalton yelled, slamming the steering wheel with his fist.

"It's a scouting group," Sam assumed.

"Should we take 'em out?" McCann asked.

"Shit. If we do, the others will come after us. I'm sure they've already radioed ahead," Dalton said.

"If we don't, we'll have to deal with them and their buddies another day," Dutch warned.

"All right. Anyone get an exact visual count?"

"No, I only saw the one," Sam said.

"I heard three different weapons," Dutch said. "If we're going to do this, we gotta do it now, Dalton."

"Kid," Dalton said to McCann, looking at him in the rearview mirror, "you're with me and Steven. Dutch, you're with Sam. Let's flank this block and head west. Get up high where you can see; let's get this over with quick and get the hell out of here. I didn't expect to find them so fast this far north. We're screwed."

The five men separated into their designated groups, and while Sam and Dutch flanked to the right of the block, the other three went to the rear of the building.

A patch of spruce trees behind the building provided them with some extra cover. They ran to the next building with weapons drawn—Dalton in front, McCann in the middle, and Steven at the rear. From there they could see Dutch and Sam peeking around the opposite side and through the narrow alleyway in between.

Dalton motioned for the others to climb the next building, and then he and his crew would go one more block before climbing a bank building while the others covered them.

When Sam gave them the signal to go, Dalton checked around the corner and scurried through an empty parking lot to the next building. As he turned to usher McCann to come, he lost all the breath left his lungs.

What Sam couldn't see was that below him stood an enemy; not the one they were afraid of, but one just as dangerous. Dalton stumbled backward and turned quickly before a large brown bear charged their position. Steven pulled McCann backward and they ran just in time.

The surreal moment began as they all watched helplessly as the ravenous bear stormed after Dalton. The carnivore lumbered toward him and shook its head left to right, opened its jaws and growled. The giant dinner-plate-sized paws slapped the ground in front of Dalton. There was no easy access ladder to climb as an escape. Dalton tried a door to one of the buildings and found it locked. The prey was trapped, and the bear seemed to know this.

Sam ran forward, leaped to the next building, and took a shot behind the beast's shoulder. They all knew their cover was blown, but he calculated the risks, and the bear would be on top of Dalton within the next half second. This was his only chance to shoot without wounding Dalton in the process.

The bear turned, distracted for a moment, after the bee-sting shot, but the wound only pissed it off more. Sam aimed and fired a second time, but the bear had already turned its aggression toward Dalton again.

Dalton gave up trying to escape, resigned himself to fight the approaching animal, and turned his weapon on it, face-to-face. He aimed and fired, knowing full well the bear would engulf him next. The animal was too large and smelled of a distinct musk he would not soon forget. Surreally he accepted that in the next instant he'd be mauled, but he wasn't about to become easy prey for the bastard.

Instantly the animal plunged into Dalton's body, pinning him against the brick building, and roared. Dalton heard shooting all around him as the bear attempted to gnaw on his head. He attempted to block the animal with his left arm and grabbed the fur on the left of its muzzle. He tried to hold the jaws away from him while he threw fist after fist, with his right arm, into the animal's jaw. All the while, claws ravaged through his tactical gear and his shoulder. Dalton pushed the massive paw away just long enough to grab his knife out of his sheath with his right arm. He rammed the blade into the bear's throat repeatedly with every ounce of strength he had left, but the animal still showed no sign of weakening. The gunfire continued, and for a moment Dalton's only thought was, *Why isn't this damn bear dead yet?*

Then, finally, the animal pulled away from him and turned to his right. Dalton slumped down, seeing only the red rush of blood. He hoped it came from the bear, but he had a sinking feeling some of it was his own. Blackness overtook his vision, and the last thing Dalton saw, as he tried to pull up his handgun to fire again, was a man clad in black pointing his own rifle at him.

Sam focused on the bear and tried to get a clean shot without wounding Dalton in the process. Everything happened so fast. At one point, he was aware of Dutch in his peripheral vision, shooting at something to his left. Then he heard a ping sail by his right ear, and he looked away from Dalton being mauled by the bear for a moment to realize men wearing black were shooting at them, and Dutch was covering him as best he could.

Then he heard yelling down below and more rapid fire ensued as McCann came out into the open and shot one of the three assailants to the left of his position through the trees. Another figure ran for cover not far from Dalton's position around the corner of the brick building. Sam had yet to locate the third shooter; reluctantly he had to abandon killing the bear and focus on stopping the assailant from killing McCann, who was now out in the open and unguarded.

"He shot him! He shot him! He's dead," McCann yelled over the commotion as he advanced on the second shooter.

Sam saw the man behind the building aim at the boy. "McCann, get down!" he yelled. When McCann turned, Sam watched as the boy recoiled from a direct shot to his side. McCann dropped to the ground, and Sam jumped from the one-story building and ran to McCann's side.

The shooter came around from the side of the building. Sam thought either he wasn't aware of the bear around the corner or he didn't care. Then he heard Dutch yell, "Up top!"

Sam had barely glanced up when Dutch shot a surprise fourth shooter on the adjacent building, who fell and landed on the ground only a few feet away from Dalton.

Sam felt for McCann's pulse at his neck but had his eyes on the last guy, who had dropped his weapon and was now backing away from the wounded and very pissed-off bear lumbering in his direction. Dutch yelled to Sam, "Shoot?"

"No! Let the bear have him!" Sam yelled. "Get the Jeep." He didn't want to take his eyes off the bear, now ravaging its new victim. The man screamed in pain, but the worst of it was the ravenous growling of the bear after its prey.

The Jeep's engine caught Sam's attention, and as Dutch pulled it up between Dalton and Sam he dragged McCann to the cab. Sam and Dutch lifted the boy inside and sat him upright. "I'm hit? He killed him . . . Steven. Steven's dead."

Sam said, "It's a shoulder wound, kid, you'll be all right."

"Steven's dead," McCann repeated.

Sam nodded. He wasn't sure yet, but he figured the kid was right. He left him there and went around to Dutch, who was bent over Dalton's mangled, bloody body.

"He alive?" Sam asked.

"He's got a pulse, but he's lost a lot of blood, man."

"Let's get him inside," Sam said, and they each took one side of Dalton, suddenly aware that the screams from the bear's new victim had subsided. They lifted Dalton's unconscious, bloody body, not knowing the extent of his injuries, and laid him across McCann's lap.

"Oh Jesus," McCann said while he felt for Dalton's pulse, even though he himself was injured.

"One more," Sam said. They ran to the opposite side of the vehicle and retrieved Steven's body. There was no doubt he was dead as they approached him. It was a clean shot through the head. Sam now felt no mercy for the bear's victim at all.

"Son of bitch," Sam said.

"Let's bring him home," Dutch said. They picked him up, opened the back door of the Jeep, and hastily laid his body in the cargo area. Dutch grabbed the first aid kit and rode shotgun as Sam jumped into the driver's seat. They sped away from the grisly scene back in the direction they had come.

"We've got to call it in. He's gonna need some blood," McCann said from the back.

"We shouldn't use the radio," Sam said.

"He's dying! He's bleeding out!" McCann yelled.

Dutch opened up the first aid kit and turned around in the seat to lean into the back.

Sam drove with a vengeance. McCann was in a lot of pain, and grunted through it as best he could. The only thing Sam could do was get them home as fast as possible while watching his rearview mirror along the way.

"There's a lot of blood, man," Dutch said to Sam.

Sam felt liquid draining down his forehead, and brushed his arm over his brow, realizing now that it was blood. They were all covered in it, not knowing whose was whose. "Is it bright red?"

"Yes and no; there's a lot of it," Dutch said. "I'm packing the wounds. Dalton's left arm is torn up bad."

"He'll make it," Sam said, accelerating further, all the while thinking of how this must end and they must survive.

"Hey kid, stay awake. We're almost there," Dutch said, patting his cheek.

McCann kept nodding off. His left shoulder hurt like hell with the tiniest of movements and yet he couldn't stay awake. He tried to take a steady, deep breath through the pain, but it was excruciating. He looked down at Dalton's unconscious face in his lap and checked his neck for a pulse again.

"He's still hanging in there, buddy," Dutch told him.

McCann could see Dalton's lower lip had turned blue since the last time he'd looked, and he was ghostly pale. "We gotta radio ahead. Clarisse will need time to get things together. He needs blood—now."

Dutch looked at the boy. "Buddy, we're going as fast as we can."

McCann shook his head, lifted Dalton's hand with his right hand, and showed him Dalton's fingernails. "See that? See how his nail bed is blue, just like his lips? He's going into shock. His pulse is weaker, and he's going to die of heart failure before we even get him there." McCann leaned back. It was excruciating to even talk or think. Then he had an idea. *He needs adrenaline to constrict his blood vessels. That'll slow the bleeding. What do we have with adrenaline?*

"Do we . . . do we have an EpiPen in that kit?"

"He's not having an allergic reaction," Dutch said, looking at McCann as if he'd lost his mind.

"It's basically adrenaline. It'll buy him some time," McCann struggled to say. Dutch rummaged around the kit and finally produced a paper-wrapped stick with EPIPEN labeled on the side.

"Give me that." McCann reached for the stick, tore the paper off with his teeth, and bit the cap off. He then plunged the needle into Dalton's thigh. He reached again for Dalton's pulse, then leaned

157

backward into the seat, trying to cope with his own pain. He felt the thrumming pulse pick up its cadence.

"It's better, but it won't last for long. I'm telling you, we need to call ahead and have her get everything ready." McCann stared Dutch in the eyes, and then focused on Sam's gaze in the rearview mirror, looking back at him. "He won't make it, Sam. He needs every advantage. You either bring him to Clarisse dead or prepare her now to save his life."

"Do it. Take the risk," Sam said to Dutch.

"You sure, man? They'll be monitoring everything for sure now," Dutch said.

Sam nodded. "Tell her we're about fifteen minutes out."

McCann leaned back, satisfied he'd made them listen to reason. His eyelids closed as he heard the chatter of Rick's voice and succumbed to sleep as Dutch relayed their horrific news.

"No, don't. I want to do it alone. He was *my* brother," Rick said as Reuben and Mark approached him at the edge of the forest line, where one large madrone tree stood separate from the others. He watched as their shadows retreated.

It was already dusk, with the remnants of shadow light cast behind him. Rick brushed the sweat from his brow and continued to dig his friend's grave. Steven lay in a blanket-covered mound to the right of the hole.

Rick caught glimpses of him each time he came up with another shovel load, until finally he knew the opening was deep enough. He stopped and grabbed the end of the shovel handle with both hands and leaned his weight onto it in a sudden surge of horrendous grief. He cried, and tears mixed with the dirt of a loved-one's grave. "Goddammit, you couldn't fucking duck?" he yelled at Steven. Great sobs followed. "You shit! I loved you, man!"

It was dark now. All lingering light had vanished and somewhere in his mind, he knew it was crazy to talk to himself and argue with dead Steven, but he did it anyway. He climbed out of the grave and continued ranting as he tugged the blanket-wrapped corpse.

"You just had to go and get yourself killed. Who the hell is going to put up with my shit now? You careless bastard." He dragged him, head first, over to the hole and jumped back inside. "It's up to me to bury your ass." He broke down again. *"Goddamn you!"* Great wracking sobs burst from Rick as he clenched Steven's body and buried his face in its side.

After the wave of grief passed, he wiped his nose with his sleeve. "I'll get them, buddy. I promise you, man." He hefted Steven into the grave and lowered him down to the cool, soft, loamy earth below in the pitch dark of night. He turned on a small flashlight and opened the blanket to look at his friend one last time, with a perfect hole blown through his forehead; Rick turned away briefly and spit dirt out of his mouth. He pulled off the chain of dog tags from around Steven's neck while bent over in the grave. A line of snot threatened to descend, and he quickly wiped it away with the back of his hand and managed to rip one of the metal tags off the ring. Then he crouched down and removed one of Steven's tags, replacing that one with one of his own. He pulled the dog tags down to Steven's chest and slipped the metal under his shirt. He put Steven's on his own chain and patted it down.

"I will never forget you, man," Rick said before refolding the blanket over his face. Taking in a deep breath as an attempt to swallow the sorrow, Rick's voice broke as he said, "Shit, this sucks." Then he climbed out of the hole one last time.

"Good-bye, Steven. You were more a brother to me than anyone. I'll miss you." He gasped for another deep breath as he took up the shovel again and spilled the soil in, slowly at first, and then it became a war. He knew he had to bury him and get it over with, or he'd completely lose his mind in grief then and there. Over and over the soil found its place in the hole once again. With the moon high overhead, Rick finally finished and mounded what was left over. He knelt and smoothed out the dirt with his hands, crumbling larger soil clods into tiny particles. He leaned back on his heels with his dirt-crusted hands laid out on his thighs.

"God, please accept my friend here. He can be a total asshole at times, but he's a good man. I also ask that you help us annihilate these fuckers. In Jesus' name, I pray. Amen." He got to his feet and picked up his shovel. "Rest, buddy," he said, and in the dark of night, he headed slowly toward the light beckoning from camp.

"McCann, McCann." Graham patted his cheek and lifted up one of his eyelids. "Son," he called to him again.

"Give him some more time. He's dreaming," someone else said, but the voice trailed away.

It's true, he dreamed. He dreamed a nightmare, only it was a memory now.

Again, he stood against the wall where Steven had shoved him out of the line of fire. It sounded like a war. A war where someone invited a bear and no one knew which side he was on. McCann found a good-sized rock on the ground near his position against the wall. It filled his palm and the weight of it was perfect. He pulled away from the building and chucked it hard as hell in the direction of the bear, hitting it squarely in the back of the head. The bear pulled up from Dalton, but then another man jumped out and fired in their direction. Steven shoved McCann down to the ground, and when McCann moved he felt only Steven's dead weight atop him. Steven was dead.

He sat up and turned him over. Steven was caught with his blue eyes open wide, still staring at the horror they found themselves in. He pushed Steven's lids closed, and anger surged up within him. He charged forward and . . .

"McCann, wake up, buddy," Graham said again and pushed on his right shoulder. "You've got to wake up, son."

"I'm here," McCann said with a heavy voice. He couldn't yet open his eyes. He left the nightmare behind for now and felt Graham trying to lift his head a little.

"Come on buddy, wake up," Graham demanded again.

"Why?" McCann said. He wasn't ready to face the world. He didn't want to dream that dream again, but somehow he thought he might be able to change the outcome if he went back into it.

"Because Clarisse said so, and believe me, it's better I wake you than if she does," Graham said.

McCann huffed; it felt like tiny anvils were holding his eyelids down.

"I just can't open them. I'm tired, man. Come back later," McCann murmured.

"Here, take a sip." Graham held a cup of water up to McCann's lips, and then he was able to finally flutter his eyes open a little sliver. As he sat up he flexed the wrong muscles in his left shoulder and pain shot through him.

"Damn, that hurts," McCann complained.

"Don't move your arm; I'll help," Graham said. He slid his arm around McCann's chest and supported his shoulder to pull him up into a sitting position as McCann used his right arm to maneuver his weight upward.

"That hurts like hell," he said and looked at his shoulder for the first time. It was all bandaged up.

"What the hell happened?" McCann asked.

Graham regarded him while he straightened his covers. "What do you remember?"

McCann shook his head, trying to clear away the grogginess. "I was shot. Dalton was attacked by a bear, and Steven—Steven's dead because of me." His voice cracked, and he looked away from Graham.

"That's not the way Sam and Dutch tell it," Graham said.

"If I hadn't . . . if I hadn't thrown the rock at the bear, Steven wouldn't have had to push me down. He'd be alive," McCann said. He couldn't hold back a sob.

"McCann," Graham lowered his voice. "Sam said the bear only turned away from Dalton when you used the rock. They shot the damn thing several times without even getting his attention. Dalton would be dead had you not intervened."

"Dalton made it?" McCann looked up at him with watery eyes.

"Yeah, he did, and it looks like you were right. The epinephrine saved his life, McCann. He nearly bled to death."

McCann wiped away his tears and took a deep breath. "Okay. I must have passed out after that." He shook his head, trying to make sense of it all.

"You did. When you guys showed up, we were all ready to do what was needed and we got Dalton into surgery right away. Unfortunately, Macy found you in the backseat with blood all over you. She's pretty freaked out. She stayed with you until we took you into surgery too, then she disappeared."

"Shit. Where is she?" McCann said, starting to move.

"It's okay; I found her in the woods. She's just scared," Graham said.

McCann nodded, knowing that he must have been a horrific sight for Macy to see. Then he remembered with urgency why they should all be afraid.

"Wait. How long has it been? How long have I been here?"

"One night. It's the next day," Graham told him.

"Have you guys heard anything from the invaders?"

"Not yet. We're monitoring all communications. We've moved everyone here to the prepper camp until we figure out what kind of threat they are. Safety in numbers."

McCann nodded. "What about the horses?"

"They're all here. Dutch and I took a truck over last night and packed up almost everything," Graham said. "You're good. Bullet went right through. You only needed a minor repair. Clarisse said that after she cleaned out the wound, she packed it with gauze. We'll need to change that out every day, but it should heal up well on its own. You were lucky."

"Okay, I need to see Macy. Can you send her to me?"

Graham shook his head. "She won't come, McCann. I tried already. She needs some time; she thought you were dead."

McCann got his first good look at Graham, who looked like death warmed over. "Have you even slept, Graham? You look awful."

"I've been right here the whole time since you came out of surgery. I tell you, it would have killed me if you hadn't made it," Graham admitted.

"I'm fine, Graham. You're not going to get rid of me that easily. How's Rick taking Steven's death?"

Graham looked out the plastic window of the tent and then down at the ground before he answered. "He buried him last night, by himself. He wouldn't let anyone help. We're going to have a ceremony for him later today. You know, I almost feel sorry for those bastards," Graham said. The vengeful lowered tone of his voice reverberated in McCann's spine, giving him chills, because Graham rarely showed hatred. He hadn't thought the man was capable of feeling it, but now he knew differently.

"Scumbags," McCann said. "And you know there are no words to describe how evil these jihad extremists are . . . what they've done."

"Perhaps that's it. They're so low beyond humanity, no name for one of their kind should ever be uttered," Graham said.

"Well, until we wipe them clean from the earth, we'll have to refer to them as something. My father called them the Malefic Nation. It means people of harm and destruction."

"I can't think of a more fitting definition, for lack of anything better, and yet it's still not low enough," Graham said.

McCann slid his legs off the bed. "Can you hand me my pants?"

"Where do you think you're going?" Graham asked.

McCann flashed a mischievous smile. "I need to clean up and then find Macy. She's not getting away from me that easily."

Graham chuckled and handed McCann a set of clothes. "I brought you some clean ones. We had to burn the others. You were soaked in your own blood, Dalton's blood . . . and the bear's, I think."

McCann lifted the sheet and clamped it back down to his side. Then a sudden horror struck him. "Wait. No. Who cleaned me up?"

Graham shrugged. "I don't know. I assume Clarisse did. She and Lucy did most of the medical work."

"Awe, man!" McCann said when he looked under his sheet again and realized he was buck naked.

Clarisse slipped back into Dalton's room. Lucy was bent over, picking up all the bloody towels and equipment they'd used and discarded while fixing him—the patching back together of what was salvageable with what was left over. It was now a matter of time, and guarding against infection. Dalton could still die on her. She knew the risks, and that's why when she left the room to make sure McCann was coming out of anesthesia on time, she'd left as a surgeon. Now she was returning as—what, Dalton's lover? It was more than that; she knew they both felt they were more than mere lovers, even though neither of them owned up to a vocal definition.

He lay there, helpless with monitors doing their work, flashing lights and beeping displays making all the right sounds.

"I think I got them all. I'll go throw them on the fire pit," Lucy said to her.

"Ah, thank you, Lucy. Go and disinfect again afterward, like I showed you, and then get yourself something to eat. Thank you for all your help today." Clarisse managed a smile as Lucy brushed past her.

She still had to tell Dalton's boys. Rick's family had them for now, and she'd asked to break the news to them herself when she was able, but the task weighed on her conscience.

"Damn you, Dalton," she whispered. It was more in anger that she cared so deeply for him and knew it would kill her if he died. He'd made her care for him; he'd made her vulnerable. He stampeded into her heart and took over somehow when she wasn't guarding it. She wasn't even sure of when it had happened.

One small step after another, she found herself at his bedside, running her fingertips over the green wool army blanket along the form of his legs. She had barely been able to repair the artery in his left shoulder. She figured he must have tried holding back the bear with that arm, because he sustained what looked like several abhorrently deep fang bites and ripping wounds.

Clarisse clasped her mouth to contain a loud cry that was threatening to escape her as she imagined what he'd been through; the tears already rolled unbridled.

His right hand . . . she knew what had happened there. The skin covering his knuckles was pared down to the white bone. He had fought for his life with that fist; she had no doubt.

"Dalton . . ." Clarisse curled the fingers of her own right hand and ran the softer skin lightly across his bare chest, where some of the bear's sharp claws had left deep marks. "Don't leave me, damn you," she whispered. It was the only sign of weakness she'd ever uttered, and even then only at a whisper. Suddenly, imagining life without Dalton tore her down. And then Rick rounded the corner.

"How's he doin'?"

She wiped away the evidence quickly before she looked up at him. "Um, better—according to the machines, anyway; he should be waking up anytime now."

"I'll wait here with him if you want to go tell the boys," said Rick. "They don't know what's going on."

She turned to Rick and was about to respond when she noticed his bloodshot eyes and the drawn expression of utter shock.

"Rick, I'm so sorry about Steven," she said, touching his forearm in comfort.

Rick shook his head in disbelief. "I just can't believe it still. This can't be real. I buried him myself, and I still can believe he's gone," he said, choking on the last word.

"Why don't you go take some time, Rick?"

"No. No, I'm fine. You need me here. I'd rather you tell the boys than me having to break the news to them. I can't, Clarisse. I just can't tell them right now. They should hear it from you, anyway."

She nodded and opened her arms wide to hug Rick, something she had never offered before.

He looked at her strangely and then shook his head again while he embraced her.

"We'll get through this, too, Rick. What doesn't kill you makes you stronger, right? That's what my mother always used to say; though I never believed her," Clarisse said, patting him on the back.

He pulled away to face her. "That's not helping, but nice try."

She teared up again, and pinched the bridge of her nose under her glasses to try to stem the flow. Rick moved to the chair next to Dalton.

"So, call you if any alarms go off, right?" Rick asked, waving his hands at the various monitors that clicked and beeped.

"Yes. Call me if he wakes up, too. I won't be long."

Lucy tossed the last of the blood-soaked towels onto the burn pit. She parsed them out, a few at a time to keep from smothering the flames. Sam had warned her not to put too much on at once so that the fire didn't produce too much smoke and draw attention to the preppers' camp. She gazed through the flames and wiped her brow with the back of her hand; she was in a trance, with people coming and going in muted colors in her peripheral vision.

It was good to work and to keep busy helping others. Lucy wanted nothing more than hard work to help the others and as little personal interaction as possible to keep herself from remembering things.

Then, through the blur, she noticed something odd as a horse moved backward. She blinked and tried to make sense of the scene.

McCann, who had just been in the infirmary on a gurney, was attempting to mount his horse—with one arm in a sling. She stood back from the fire to get a better look at his feeble attempts. He pulled the line back into position with his right hand and clasped the mount while holding the lead line. Then he put his left boot into the stirrup and seemed to sway, losing his balance. The horse looked confused and took a step sideways, screwing up McCann's plan altogether.

"Dammit," McCann said with subtle impatience.

Lucy looked from side to side in hopes someone would come along and stop him from his own foolishness, but at that moment no one was anywhere in sight. She picked up her basket and walked reluctantly toward him as he tried again to mount the horse with the use of only his right arm, again failing miserably.

Coming up behind McCann, she asked, "Should you be doing that?"

He turned around to see who was talking to him, and then answered, "I've got something to do."

"You just woke from surgery. Does Clarisse even know you're out here?"

McCann gave up for a second and turned to Lucy with a huff. "Hey, can you please do me a big favor and hold the line?" He held out the rope for her to take.

She looked down at the rope and shook her head. "No. I'll get in trouble. You're not supposed to be riding. I don't think you're even supposed to be walking."

"It's okay, really. You won't get in any trouble. Here, take it," he said, thrusting the rope out to her again.

Lucy still didn't take it. "Look. Can I go and get whatever it is you need?"

He looked at her, frustrated. "No. You can't. Please just hold the line so he'll stay in position. I won't tell anyone you helped me, I promise."

Lucy looked around her again, and when she turned toward him, she jumped back automatically after seeing he held the line too close to her. She gasped and dropped the basket she had held, now enclosing herself in her arms, fighting her own inner demons.

"Hey, I'm sorry. I'm sorry," McCann repeated twice, holding up his right hand. "I didn't mean to scare you."

She pulled back the long strands of red hair that had fallen into Lucy's face.

"It's . . . It's okay. I'm fine," Lucy said, trying to convince herself that she was, in fact, all right.

"No, I'm sorry. That was foolish of me. Honestly, no one is going to harm you here. You don't need to be scared. I'm just in a hurry."

Lucy put on a slight smile, knowing that McCann was only trying to make her feel better. "Okay, just hurry. I don't want to be on Clarisse's bad side."

"You and me both," he mumbled. He handed her the line, keeping his own hand far away from hers.

"Do I hold it taut if he bucks?"

McCann smirked. "He won't buck. He's just not used to me without a left arm to use."

"See, even *he* knows you're not supposed to be doing this," Lucy said. She took another look around to make sure the coast was clear while McCann got into position to take another stab at it, failing miserably once more. He staggered before he caught his balance this time.

"Hey, aren't you on Vicodin?" she asked.

"Is that what you guys gave me? Dammit, I've got to find her. Hang on, one more try." He kicked over a nearby feed bucket with his boot and scooted it into position.

Lucy laughed at McCann's determination. He got close to the horse and put his left foot on top of the bucket in preparation to launch himself up and onto the saddle. With his left arm in a sling, she figured that—despite the Vicodin—this had to hurt like hell.

Before she could warn him, McCann launched himself again and landed with his torso across the saddle, but without quite getting his right knee high enough to gain traction. Instead he hung there.

At that moment, Sam came out of the stable, and Lucy shrunk, knowing she was now in big trouble. Sam stopped his stride and looked at the two of them, assessing the situation; Lucy holding the rope and McCann across the mare, ass up, with a surprised look on his face.

"He's . . . trying to get on the . . . the horse," Lucy stuttered. "I tried to stop him, but he won't listen to me, and he's high on Vicodin."

"Sam. Sam, I gotta find her," McCann said as a means of explaining his side of the story.

Lucy watched as Sam took in the scene and seemed to make a judgment on the predicament before him. He walked within five feet

173

of the young man and the horse, then pushed McCann's right knee up so that he could get into the saddle. Then he took the reins from Lucy and handed them up to McCann once he was upright in the saddle.

"She's in the woods by the stream. I never saw you," Sam said and walked off without another word.

Lucy only stared.

"This"—McCann slurred, motioning his right hand in a circle—"did not happen."

Lucy watched him ride away toward the river. "I hope he doesn't fall and break his neck," she said under her breath, again looking to see if there were any witnesses. Then she hurried back to the infirmary.

Clarisse passed Lucy in the hallway but avoided making eye contact.

"Make sure you get dinner, Lucy. I'll see you back at our tent later tonight. I'll probably stay with Dalton for a while. Will you be okay alone?"

"Yes, Clarisse, of course; I'll sit with Addy and Sam at dinner like last time. Please let me know if there's anything more I can do."

"You've been a great help already. I thank God you were here. We were already running pretty thin before this happened."

"Again, don't hesitate let me know if there is anything else I can do," Lucy reiterated.

"Well, just say hi to Addy for me. I feel like I haven't seen her in days."

"I will. Bye!"

Clarisse started to walk away, but remembered something and turned. "Oh, Lucy. Have you seen McCann? I need to talk to him about stepping in for Steven, since he has some medical knowledge, but when I checked his room he'd already left."

"Uh . . . nope," Lucy answered sheepishly.

Clarisse thought Lucy looked nervous, but dismissed it as part of Lucy getting over her trauma and meeting so many new people. "No big deal. If you see him, please send him to me. Thank you."

"I will," Lucy said, scurrying off with her head down.

Clarisse walked on and took a deep breath as she exited the infirmary tent into the evening air. The light was only just beginning to subside, and she loved that the sunlight of day stretched longer and longer this time of year. She could smell something coming from the mess tent and thought it might be a casserole. The scent smelled comforting, and these days they needed all the comfort they could get.

As Clarisse passed through the main yard, she saw Mark and Marcy up on the guard stand alongside another guard from the prepper camp. It was great to have Graham's camp here among them; at least she wouldn't have to worry about them being out there on their own. That, and she could keep a better eye on Tala, who did not have much longer to go before the birth.

They just needed to remain quiet and undetected as much as possible in order to get by. Clarisse hoped they would all be able to stay in their camp for now, but she knew that Graham, Reuben, and Rick were planning a contingency to bug out at a moment's notice. The idea of leaving wasn't so comforting, especially when the leader of the group was in the infirmary and they had children and a pregnant woman to consider, but this was life now, and they had to do whatever it took to survive.

Despite the almost cheerful evening walk to Rick's family's tent, each step brought on a foreboding sense of dread. On one hand, Clarisse could tell the boys a bear had attacked their father and he sustained many injuries and he could die still; that was the truth. On the other, she could tell the boys their father was in surgery due to bear attack injuries and he was recovering nicely. She still hadn't made a decision, and she was only five steps from their tent door.

She stopped on the third step and put her hands on her narrow hips, looking down in thought, kicking the dust up with her combat boot. These boys were still coping with the loss of their mother; they had been told their dad was in the infirmary but nothing more. "Just tell them the truth," she finally said to herself. She shook her doubts away, lifted her head, pushed her glasses in place, and closed the gap.

"Hi, Olivia," she said to Rick's wife, who was sitting in a chair reading a book. Clarisse was taken aback by the grief apparent on Olivia's face, but losing Steven was like losing a brother to Rick's family, and Clarisse had almost forgotten that. "I'm sorry, Olivia," she said.

"Oh, we all are, Clarisse. It's so hard, knowing it could be anyone at any minute. We all survived the pandemic and, for a while, we thought that would be it. But it's not. We're still vulnerable. It could have easily been Rick. He would have been the one to go on the scouting mission if he hadn't been shot in the leg the day before. This is never going to end, this feeling that any second my husband will die . . . or my Bethany. Sorry, I'm just still in shock."

Clarisse walked farther into the darkened tent and could hear what sounded like a cartoon on in the next room. She sat on a chair next to Olivia and placed her hand on her shoulder. "You're grieving, and all the *could haves* are normal to feel right now. It's fear that has saved us all, and it's fear and determination that will continue to save us. Steven's loss is a real blow. I don't know what I'm going to do without him, frankly." She stared out in silence for a second, remembering the time she had walked in on him playing with the test ferrets like puppies one day, looking up at her with a goofy grin. "God, he used to drive me crazy." She sniffed and wiped an errant tear from under her glasses.

"I don't know what we're going to do," Clarisse continued. "One thing at a time, I guess. Right now, I've got to tell Dalton's two little boys that their dad isn't out of the woods yet, and so soon after losing their mom. I've got to do this and get back to him. I hope you don't mind."

"Of course not. I hope he recovers quickly. We need him," Olivia said.

"I need him. I know that now. Come talk to me anytime, Olivia. We're both so busy holding up our own ends that it seems I never get to see you."

"I'd like that. They're in Bethany's tent watching *Pocahontas* again. I wish we'd packed more movies; that one is driving me nuts.

177

It's all they ever watch, but I think when things start to get a little uncertain again, the kids want to zone out on what they know, something comforting from the old world," Olivia chuckled.

"I'll just chat with them a minute and then head back, if that's okay."

"Of course," Olivia said, turning back to her book.

Clarisse got up and walked nearer to the musical notes coming from the other tent room. When she rounded the corner she saw three children lying on their bellies, propping their little heads up on their hands with their elbows pointed into the vinyl ground.

"Hi guys," Clarisse said, slipping down to sit beside them. She sat crossed-legged and caressed Kade along his back. All three heads turned in unison and smiled at her, then turned back to the movie.

"Bethany, can you come in here please," they heard Olivia call from the other room. Bethany scooted up and stepped over the boys while leaving the room.

"Hey, guys. I need to talk to you," Clarisse said. "Can I have you sit up for a minute?"

Hunter, the older of the two at six, looked up at her, glanced back to the show for a moment, then pulled his eyes away again and sat up. "Is it about Dad?" he asked.

"Yes."

That got Kade's attention too, and they both sat up and pulled their legs into the same position as Clarisse's. She couldn't help but smile at their sweet faces. She reached over, placing one hand on each of their far shoulders. She smiled reassuringly. The pit of her stomach suddenly turned to stone. "Your d—"

"Is he dead?" Hunter asked, interrupting her words in a deadpan voice. The blow scared Clarisse, and she dropped her hands from their shoulders.

"No—no. He's coming out of recovery, Hunter." She suddenly realized, even at six, this young man had seen and been through too much. "He was attacked by a bear," she said quietly and waited for a reaction.

"Is he okay?" Kade asked. His big eyes teared up while Hunter looked sullen and picked at his boot.

"He's uncon . . . he's sleeping right now. I performed surgery to fix him back up. It might take him a long time to get better."

"Did the bear bite him?" Kade asked.

"Of course it did, Kade," Hunter said in anger.

Clarisse waited a second to pass before she formulated an answer. "The bear bit his shoulder, and he lost a lot of blood, but he will get better." Her stomach clenched when she caught herself in this untruth. She didn't know yet if Dalton would get better, but she couldn't look into his sons' eyes and tell them he might die. She had thought she could, but not now.

"Can I see him?" Kade asked in his high-pitched little boy voice.

Clarisse smiled and tried to hold back emotion as she detected resilience in Kade's voice. "He's not ready yet for visitors, but I will come and get you as soon as he is. Okay?"

Kade nodded and Hunter mumbled, "He's probably gonna die, anyway, just like Mom."

"Don't say that, Hunter!" Kade yelled, and he began to weep.

"Don't cry, Kade. It's all right," Clarisse said. She slid him onto her lap and hugged him. She kissed the top of his head, which smelled like little boy sweat as he leaned into her. "Let me tell you both something. Your dad is not going to die. But even if he did, you know that Rick and I would always take care of you." She laid her right hand on Hunter's knee. "You'll never be alone. I promise you that."

Clarisse knew that she hadn't told the whole truth, but she also knew she would try her hardest to have Dalton survive this, no matter what. These boys needed their father, and she was going to do everything she could to make sure they kept him.

"Do you understand, Hunter?" she asked the sullen boy.

He grimaced, but flashed her his sad eyes and agreed.

She held Kade tightly and then kissed him again. "I've got to get back to your dad now. I'll check on you guys later and bring you any news. Okay?"

They nodded, and she slid the youngest child off her lap and stood up. Both boys returned to their previous positions on their bellies to watch the screen and zone out once again. With the hardships of their current reality, she hoped they'd gain some peace in an imaginary one.

Clarisse stopped the door flap before exiting and remembered her promise to them. She wiped the moisture from her eyes on the way out and waved good-bye to Olivia and Bethany on her way back to the infirmary, hoping she'd done the right thing.

"Where've you been, Sam?" Reuben asked as Sam appeared in the media tent for his turn on watch, only a few minutes late.

"I got a little sidetracked on the way," Sam said, and Graham waited for the reason, but Sam didn't offer one. Instead, he was busy bringing in what looked like spools of drab-green paracord on sticks of various sizes, as well as a hatchet.

"So, you're on watch now. I'll go relieve the guard for dinner," Reuben said.

"I can take a turn too, Reuben," Graham said.

"We need you here until Rick's back. We need two people as runner and listener in case we hear or see something on camera," Reuben explained.

Graham agreed with that logic, and then Sam said, "Hey, Reuben before you leave, make sure McCann and Macy are back by dark. If they're not, let me know."

"Where'd McCann go?" Graham asked as Sam unrolled large lengths of the paracord on the ground between his knees.

"He's on a mission. He's fine. Guy's gotta do what a guy's gotta do." Sam pulled out his pocket knife and cut off a precise length of cord, tying a knot on the opened end.

"Gotcha. Graham said, snickering and let it lie, knowing what McCann was up to but concerned about his condition all the same. What are you making?"

"Traps," Sam said, but nothing more.

"Wait, is McCann mounted?" Reuben called from the door.

"Yeah. He's mounted," Sam said, and Reuben left to resume his other duties.

After Reuben left, Sam said, "I don't envy you. Two daughters . . ." He looked up at Graham and shook his head as if the condition were the worst plague ever imagined.

"Yeah, but this is nothing." He watched Sam cut off two more lengths of cording about the same length of the first. "At least they aren't fighting right now. That drives me crazy. Tala's good with them, though."

"How's she getting along with the move? Sorry we had to pull you guys over here, but it's for the best," Sam said with a strand in his mouth.

"She's a trooper. She's got everything worked out. Nothing rattles her too much . . . except for the idea of me getting killed, that is," Graham admitted.

"Yeah, losing Steven has been a real blow, and having Dalton this far gone really has us at a disadvantage. He'll come through it though—out of pure will if nothing else. He won't leave those boys if he can help it." Sam laid the paracord lengths to the side to pick up the hatchet and a sturdy V-shaped stick. He started to cut a notch below the V.

Graham got the intensity of Sam's statement, but he still worried about Dalton as their leader. With Rick compromised over the loss of Steven, this group would go astray without Dalton's leadership. They had the tactical power to fight off a large group, but being short on men had them at a disadvantage. Graham scanned the cameras again while Sam worked on what he could only guess was a snare of some kind.

"What's the contingency, Sam? If we hear from them, that is."

"Depends on what they do and how close they get," Sam said. "If they track us here, we've got to fight them and run for it. We've got the vehicles with provisions all ready and a route planned north to bug out. We're hidden here, but not that well hidden. It's a matter of time. We've got to go after them before they discover us. Right now, we're sitting ducks. That's not a good position to be in."

"Have you ever been a police officer or a soldier, Sam?"

"No, but I've fought man, bear, and beasts of all kinds in my time. I'd count these guys in the beasts category. No man would ever be this vile. These are too far gone for redemption. They must be exterminated like the scum they are." Then he sunk the hatchet into the notch he'd just created.

Graham had never heard Sam speak more than a few sentences strung together. This kind of thinking was still new to Graham, but he had to agree. They needed to fight back and fast, but the problem was that they didn't know how widespread the invaders were. They could have been pouring into Texas and the southern borders all this time.

"I'm on board one hundred percent, Sam," Graham said.

Graham checked the cameras again in detail. The center of Cascade looked clear aside from a herd of deer munching on new spring growth near the post office.

"Did McCann look like he was stable enough to ride on his horse?" Graham asked after a moment. He watched as Sam formulated an opinion while working on the second stick. "No, but he knows what he's doing. My mother would say that boy is touched with an old soul. I wouldn't worry about that one. Mark and Marcy, on the other hand, are going to make you a pops before too long."

"Don't say that, man," Graham pleaded, holding up his hand. "I don't know what to do with those two."

"Nothing you can do. Nature tells them what to do, what's needed. Right now there's a need for more babies in the world. Problem is, we're still fighting the enemy. We're not safe yet."

Amid the surveillance camera equipment, both of their heads popped up from their tasks as the occasional repeaters operated — now with an eerie human voice erupting over the waves. Their eyes met. It was a voice of normality from the past stating the frequency and call of the programmed repeaters, still announcing its duty in a world with few men left to care about it. It teased them. Sam shook his head in fervent hatred and Graham nodded, looking past him in resigned agreement.

It was the forest again. Her smell lingered among the shadowed pines. Once he entered, the sunset glimmered through the high trees alerting McCann to the time; too few minutes remained before it would set. He gently called to her, "Maaacy."

Only silence filled the air, leaving it bereft of her. McCann tempted her with another soft call. The drugs were impairing his senses, but he felt her here, he knew her presence.

Then a chance sunset ray caught a strand of her golden hair behind a tree trunk. He searched further and found her peeking out at him with one blue eye.

"Macy."

"What are you doing here?" she said.

"Looking for you."

She leaned out from the tree, using one hand for leverage to look at him wholly. "You're crazy," she said, somewhat flattered that McCann had come looking for her in his condition.

"Come, Macy. Don't make me get down. I don't know if I'll be able to get back up," he admitted, holding his right arm out for her as if she'd obey him that easily.

"I want to go home. Not there," she complained.

"It is our home for now. It's safer, Macy. Come here, please," he coaxed further.

She shot behind the tree again and out of sight.

"Dammit, Macy. Come here," he said, swaying in his saddle, his head spinning while he looked for her in the dimming light.

"Go back, McCann. I'll come in later. When I want to."

He got more frustrated; light was sinking farther down through the pines. Her voice seemed to be moving around him.

"Macy, please, come to me," he pleaded, knowing the stern voice would never do with her. He waited, hoping she'd have mercy on him. He closed his eyes to the dusk and tried to listen for her. Moments passed and no alert came to him. He took a deep breath, knowing he'd have to dismount to find her. He blew the breath out with control, steadily, needing to pull as much patience from the act as possible.

"Okay, I'm coming for you," he said in final resignation, lifting his boot to dismount. A light grasp on his thigh shocked him through. Macy's blue eyes pierced McCann with what little golden flickers remained of the descending sun. He gave her his right arm, steady and strong. She embraced it and used her knee as leverage against the horse's side as he pulled her up and settled her in front of him in the saddle.

"You should probably drive, sneaky," he said. He handed her the reigns, and then wrapped his arm around her waist and whispered into the back of her neck, "Don't worry, Macy. I'd never leave you."

Dalton's chest rose and fell with a cadence that Rick's own breathing began to emulate. "Come on, Dalton. Wake up, man. I've got crap to do."

Rick tossed his hat a few more times, letting the circumference loop through his hands while he stared down between his knees. The silence, interrupted only by mechanical beeping, was driving him nuts. "Seriously, a lot of shit is going on, man. I'm not sure we can do this without you." He slid his hand over his own tired face, the skin still rough and calloused from the work of grave digging.

"How's he doing?" Clarisse asked, startling Rick as she entered the room. "Any changes?"

"No. No, I don't think so."

"It's okay. You can get back now. I've told the boys."

"How'd they take the news?" he asked her.

Clarisse ran her hand over her smooth hair, making sure it was still in place. "I wanted to tell them the truth. I wanted to let them know the reality that he could still die." Remembering, she broke eye contact with Rick and looked down at the ground, shaking her head. "I couldn't do it. He's got to pull through this. He has no choice."

"He will, Clarisse," Rick said. "Yes, he has no fucking choice. Hear that, asshole?" Rick directed the message at Dalton's sleeping form, then stood and stretched.

"You should go get some sleep, Rick."

"Can't. No rest for the wicked, and I'm going to be very fucking wicked here soon," he said as he departed the tent into the evening air.

Clarisse watched him go, and felt a menacing tingle; every hair on her arms and neck stood on end. Rick was a man renowned of many unique talents. Now he was a man hell-bent on brutal annihilation, and with his mind working on the demise of another, she thought, *hell hath no mercy for those on the wrong side of vengeance.*

She shrugged off the prickles and focused on Dalton again. Scanning every machine connected to the man she loved, she was relieved that there were no changes indicating a setback of any kind. She needed to wake him now to find out if there would be any further emergencies as he gained consciousness.

Leaving Dalton's side, she walked over to close the tent flap door for privacy and then removed her glasses. "Okay, sweetheart. Time to come back to me."

A white sheet was tucked at Dalton's waistline, and Clarisse pulled it slowly down to his ankles, accessing the broken body before her and taking in the unbroken parts of him that she loved so much. She ran her hand, lightly and slowly, to the inside of his hairy, muscular thigh. She couldn't think of a better way of waking him from such a deep sleep than kissing him lightly on the lips and massaging him where she knew he loved her touch. She carefully avoided the torn shoulder, moving her other hand to his dark-blond locks and gently weaving them through her fingers.

Dalton's right hand flinched in her peripheral view after a moment, and she turned her head to the side to glance at the EKG machine, where the needle showed a slight increase in heart rate.

"Don't you dare stop now," came his husky breath to her ear.

She smiled down at him, overjoyed that he had come back to her. With tears dropping to his chest, she whispered, "I never stop what I've started. You know that about me."

Tala woke up on her side in their temporary accommodations, Graham spooning behind her, his arm draped over her swollen belly. The baby kicked and turned within her.

"*He* wants to play," Graham said sleepily into the back of her head.

"You mean *she* don't you?" Tala said as he smoothed his hand over her creamy bare skin where her tank top rode up. Then she felt his hand travel to her hip.

"Tala," he said, nuzzling in closer.

"Nope," she said and pointed to the other side of the tent where a little boy snored soundly, but not soundly enough. She put her finger to her lips and smiled teasingly up at Graham. "Shhh."

He dropped his head in defeat. "Okay, I've got to go to help out anyway," he said and swung his legs over the side of their cot.

"Me, too. I've got kitchen duty this morning."

"Take it easy, please," Graham said, tugging on his jeans.

Tala propped herself up on her elbows to watch him dress. "Did you make sure the boys were in the boys' tent and the girls were in the girls' tent last night?"

"Yes, I did, at around three this morning when I got off guard duty, but that doesn't mean anything. Sheriff was with Macy though," he said, leaving the tent for the showers.

"Have a nice day at work, Graham." Tala tormented him again with a wicked smile and a raised eyebrow, and he shot her a devilish look that said *Enough, or you'll be sorry*. She lay back down after he left, curling up where his warmth and smell still lingered on the bed. It frightened her that they couldn't feel safe in their own cabin, alone—just Tala, Graham, and the children she'd come to love and call her own.

Now the twins were in the tent set up next to theirs, and the boys were on the other side, all in a row like the rest of the preppers. There was no more making Graham coffee at dawn, or the little things that made up their morning routine. Even the kids, only on their second day at the prepper camp, were still adjusting, though they all knew it was for the best and they had to make it work for now.

"Are we going to work in the garden today?"

Tala rolled over to see Bang peeking back out at her. A blush threatened her face. She hoped he hadn't been awake long and had picked up on their playful banter. "Yes, I think so; after breakfast," she said.

Tala sat up, pulled her sweater on over her cotton tank top, and said, "Time to start the day."

Bang smiled at her. "I have to take care of the chickens. They don't like it here. They think they're lost," he said.

"Hmm," Tala said, knowing he was talking about more than the chickens. "Are you giving them the same feed?"

"Yeah," he said.

"Are you spending time with them like you used to?"

"Yeah," he said nodding.

"Well," she said and brushed his hair out of his eyes, "try talking to them and letting them know this is only temporary. It's safer here and nothing will happen to them while we have more people to guard them. Let them know that as soon as danger has passed, we will return to the cabin, but for now we have to adapt to our new circumstances."

"Are the bad men that killed Steven coming here?" Bang asked in a dropped whisper with eyes wide in fright.

Tala closed her lips in a thin line, thinking of what was best to reveal and what he didn't need to know at his age. She finally pulled his small frame to her side and said in all honesty, "We don't know yet, Bang, but we will keep you safe no matter what." That seemed to be all he was asking for, just that much reassurance. He leaned into her and she hugged him with her heart on edge.

When she left the tent with Bang, he headed off in the opposite direction toward the animal section and waved as if he was going off to school and she to work. She'd never realized how much the prepper camp was like a little city, all within the confines of a gated enclosure—except for Clarisse's quarantine lab, which was not simply a lab.

She'd hoped to hear word about Dalton's condition, and as she neared the mess hall she ran into Marcy already hard at work taking orders from Olivia. She hugged Marcy and said, "Good morning, dear."

"Good morning, Tala," Olivia said. "You didn't have to come in this early in your condition. You should sleep as much as you can. When the baby's born, forget that luxury."

"Oh, I know; it's already waking me up early, though. It's okay. I want to help out as much as I can now. Have you heard anything about Dalton?" she asked while putting on an apron.

Olivia bent over a vat of steaming oatmeal, stirring while Marcy spilled a couple handfuls of raisins into the pot. "Yes! He's awake and doing well. Rick came in last night, said Clarisse stopped by the media tent on her way in to tell him that Dalton was up and looking good. He's already out of bed. I haven't seen him yet, but Rick said Clarisse won't let him do too much yet. His shoulder's bandaged, and he's in a lot of pain, but she's taking care of him. He'll be fine."

"That's great news. We all needed that," said Tala. Then she stacked paper bowls and set up plastic spoons near the oatmeal station. Marcy was filling the large commercial coffee maker with water, and Tala set out the sugar, faux sugar packets, and stir sticks. She then looked for the powdered creamer but there was none.

"Olivia, is there more creamer somewhere?"

"Ah . . . nooo," she said with a dismayed look on her face. "We are all out of the powdered creamer, and Dalton is going to start a revolution when he finds out. I've been slipping canned evaporated milk into his coffee, which Rick came in for earlier, but we don't have much of that left either. It's black from now on, if anyone asks—until we run out of coffee itself, that is."

"God help us all when that happens," Tala said, thinking of how grumpy Graham was without his coffee.

Marcy laughed. "That's just too bad. They both need to get off caffeine anyway. It's bad for you."

Olivia stirred brown sugar into the oatmeal and tapped the large metal spoon on the side of the pot when she was through. She smiled and laughed at a memory, "Honey, you don't want to be around Rick or St—" she shuddered, stopped, and the smile dropped from her face utterly.

Tala looked at her, saddened by her obvious heartache.

"I'm sorry. It's so hard to accept he's gone," Olivia said.

Before Tala could comment, people started filtering in for breakfast. Olivia put on a bright smile through her watery eyes and welcomed them while Tala looked at Marcy, who now appeared in painful remorse too. These things couldn't be helped; they had their own sadness at Ennis's passing—even now—and they both knew that grief took time.

"I had no idea you were so devious," McCann said to Sam as they carried out the traps and lethally sharpened spears in two quivers. The knee-high sword ferns gleamed a brilliant green all around them.

"It's survival, that's all," Sam explained, setting the first trap. He then pointed out into the forest. "You see how the deer have created this natural highway through the woods? The invaders will follow this opening to avoid making unnecessary noise. We need to set up bow traps along this perimeter and camouflage them under the natural brush along the path.

"Watch how I set one of these up, and then you can help me with the rest." Sam began pounding several sticks into the ground, which he then laid a bow across. He extended the string behind the bow at full pull and pounded several more sticks into the ground at that position. Then he took a stick tied to a string and pounded it into the ground across the deer path. "This is the tripwire," he said, pounding in a few more sticks into the ground, around which he looped the string. He tied the other end of the tripwire to a tiny stick, then pulled the bowstring back, setting it behind the fulcrum stick and securing everything with the tripwire stick.

Sam leaned backward on his knees and held his hands up in warning.

"Okay, pay attention. This thing is lethal once you place the spear inside of the device. It's under a lot of pressure. The arrow will lean upward at a slight angle. There's a notch here at the end of the spear, see?" He showed McCann where the bowstring would slide smoothly inside the crevice. "Do not walk in front of the trap—for any reason—after loading the spear. We'll set these up after Rick finishes the final touches on his reapers."

McCann thought these bow traps were damned impressive alone, but he had no idea of what Rick had planned. "What the heck is a reaper?" he asked, and Sam did something McCann never expected to hear from him. It scared him.

Sam giggled low and devious, then said, "You think I've got tricks up my sleeve—Rick's a twisted, freaky fucker. He's designed this thing—I can't tell you; I'll have him explain it to you. This thing is something you have to see for yourself. Anyway, no one ventures this direction, unless of course they have a death wish to be impaled or shot—or both."

McCann cleared his dry throat. "Yeah. That's for sure."

They made their way through the forest to where Rick was perched atop their Jeep. He had hooked something over a branch and pushed it back to conceal it under the evergreen brush.

"That should do it. Last one," Rick said to them as they approached. The temperature was warm enough to cause Rick to break a sweat work, and McCann thought Rick looked as if he hadn't slept in days. His army T-shirt was drenched through as he finished the final touches on his equipment while McCann surveyed the contraption to try to figure out what it was.

"Explain to McCann how these damn things work, Rick," Sam said.

"Sure, just a second." Rick wiped the sweat from his eyes with his forearm. "The scheme really isn't that hard if you just put a few different concepts together into one project. It helped that I used to be an RC—remote control—airplane enthusiast and a gun nut.

"For the remote control functions of the gun, I used a 2.4 gigahertz RC radio system consisting of a transmitter and a receiver. The new 2.4 systems lock on to a single transmitter/receiver like a cell phone. That helps keep other radio transmissions from interfering and makes it just a little harder for the system to be hijacked. The transmitter is the controller you would fly the RC airplane with, and the receiver would normally be mounted on an airplane. The receiver takes the signals from the controller, then sends the commands to each of the servos that operate the different control surfaces of the airplane.

"I made a mounting bracket that attaches to a tree branch and hangs from underneath. The mount for the gun hangs underneath on an aluminum dual-axis mount to allow it to move on the yaw and pitch control axes. That gives the operator full range of motion of the gun with a simple joystick on a controller. There are two servos connected to the mounting bracket—one for each axis, and each axis uses the control arms that would normally move the flight control surfaces to move the gun mount underneath.

"When the operator pulls back with the controller, the barrel goes up; when he pushes forward, it goes down, left and it goes left, right and it goes right. I had to use the beefiest servos available to get it stout enough to move the way I wanted it to and to be reliable under stress, but it was worth the search.

"The weapon mounted underneath the contraption is a stripped-down M4 carbine that uses the flat-top rail on the upper receiver to mount to the control mechanism where there would normally be a sight, optic, or the old school carry handle–sight combo mounted. In the interest of saving weight, I stripped it of its stock and only have the buffer tube in place on the rear, removed the forward hand guards, and sawed the triangular front sight off, leaving only the gas block, gas tube, and a lightweight pencil profile barrel out front—no muzzle device. I also mounted a solenoid from an RC airplane alongside the magazine well to actuate the trigger that also receives input from the transmitter via the receiver. This particular M4 just happens to have a class three lower receiver with the full autofire control group installed, and is loaded with a hundred-round Beta Mag dual drum setup. I figured a hundred rounds would be plenty, since by that point this thing is liable to have shaken itself apart from the pounding of the recoil action.

"For aiming, the primary system is a camera mounted on the gun mount that transmits live video feeds to a monitor colocated with the RC transmitter. Since the camera can't actually sight in the exact path of the bullets, the Beta Mag is loaded every third round with a tracer so that the path of the bullets can actually be seen by the camera and adjusted accordingly. The tracers also work as a backup aiming system in the event of camera failure; as long as the RC transmitter operator has his eyes on the gun, he can direct the fire visually with the tracers.

"The whole setup is powered by an onsite battery pack, trickle charged via a small solar panel mounted near the top of the tree. The way I see it, the hundred rounds of ammo will be expended long before the battery, so the trickle charger is really to keep the battery topped off and ready for use—not for replenishment of a drained battery."

McCann consumed every detail, and imagined the invaders running for cover in all directions from these things. After a dead second of quiet, in awe, McCann said, "You are both tricky dudes."

"Damn straight. It's something I'm proud of," Rick said, smiling.

"The two of you scare the hell out of me. You're a crazy team," McCann said. He's always known these two guys had skills, but now he was impressed in a scared-shitless kind of way. "I think I know more now than I should," McCann admitted, brushing down the bristling hairs on the back of his neck.

Rick laughed. "Yes, this is a bit above your pay grade, I'm afraid."

There was a sudden rustling in the woods about sixty feet from their position to the south, and McCann nearly pissed his pants. He drew his Colt automatically, but the sudden jerk affected his shoulder wound and had him crouching in pain. Sam was down to the ground, bow ready, and Rick had jumped down from the Jeep to hide behind the tree he'd been working on earlier. He held his M1A pressed firmly against his cheek while looking through the Leupold scope. "Deer," Rick whispered after a moment.

"Christ, that scared the hell out of me," McCann admitted.

Sam stood cautiously and whispered, "Can't be too careful. Now it's time to turn the hunters into the hunted."

"It's not as easy as you think," Dutch tried to explain in a soft encouraging voice to Lucy, Macy, Bang, and some of the prepper children. Macy didn't think he was aware of her and Bang's level of skill, but they would show him soon enough, and even so, maybe Dutch had something to teach them. Lucy, Hunter, Kade, Bethany, and Addy stood beside them, listening intently to the instructions.

Dutch's dogs and Sheriff hung out nearby; Elsa lolled in the sparse growth of the forest floor, while Frank and Sheriff panted at their sides, acting as if they too were a part of the instructions.

"You have to launch the arrow a bit higher to account for wind and drop," he continued. "It curves as it hits the target. See? Watch, let me demonstrate it for you."

He aimed for one of the targets thirty yards away, set opposite the fence line, and began to instruct through his motions. "Elbow straight back along your line of sight, straight and level. Don't let it slop down. Bowstring just to the right of your lip center. Aim, breathe out, hold, and release." He let the arrow fly. Macy watched the red tail wiggle about in the first few milliseconds as the arrow took flight and struck the target on the ring edge, left of center.

"Now you try," he instructed them. Macy and Bang both lifted their bows fluidly, with expert skill, and sent their arrows straight into the gold center. Lucy and the others had yet to get their bows into position as the two arrows landed with soft *thunks* one a split second after the other. Dutch stopped in his tracks. "I think I've just been had!" he said, and both Macy and Bang giggled. "Why didn't you say so? Hell, *you* teach them; I've got other stuff to do," Macy raised her eyebrows at Lucy with a smirk as Dutch headed back to camp.

"He's not really grouchy," Lucy explained, waving Dutch off. "Now, can you show me how to do that?"

"Sure, but he's the one who taught me," Macy said, pointing at Bang.

"Seriously?" Lucy asked, surprised. "That's awesome."

"Okay, traps and surveillance are set. Our location is secure, for now," Dalton said to them after Rick had explained the situation.

Clarisse handed him a pain pill and a cup of water to chase it down with. He wasn't exactly mobile, but sitting up in bed, he'd called the meeting in his room. If he walked more than ten feet he'd become lightheaded, nauseated, and have to sit down again, so it worked better to have them come to him. They were all scattered around, gawking at his wounds, standing or sitting.

"We've worked out a few different contingency escape routes, just in case," Dutch said.

The men looked to Dalton for orders. They depended on him and he wasn't fit for battle. Not like this. It scared the hell out of him that he was so weak and at such a critical time. The only thing he could do was talk them through things. For now, at least, that would have to do.

"Any signals?" he asked Rick, who looked like hell himself, dark circles around his eyes. The man was pale, and Dalton had seen that look on his face before. It was a look of suppressed rage just below the surface.

Years ago in the desert, they'd lost one of their own in the worst of ways. He was a lousy soldier, but he was *their* lousy soldier and he'd gotten himself captured, the dumbass. After torturing him, the enemy had finally beheaded him, and they sent a horrific video of the entire ghastly ordeal to them.

Rick had tried in vain to locate their comrade's position before the inevitable. They'd used every shred of intel, but nothing surfaced in time. It was a devastating blow. They'd finally identified one of the assailants in the video, but not before having to watch the torture repeatedly. It turned out to be a woman jihadist.

It was an ironic discovery. The dead soldier was one of them, but he wasn't exactly the best family man. If fact, he was quite a deplorable father. They'd spent weeks afterward tracking down all six of his kids by various mothers to relay the dreaded news; turns out they didn't really seem to care if the man was alive or dead. The look on Rick's face back then wasn't anything compared to what Dalton saw now.

"A few scattered clicks came through last night. They could be fucking with us, but more than likely it was interference. Dutch and I both tried to detect any Morse code from it, but the string was too random. We think it's more likely white noise," Rick said, his voice gravely and broken.

"Okay, still, anything unusual we want to watch like hawks." Dalton looked to Reuben. "Trucks loaded and pointed in the right directions?"

"Affirmative. Extra caches also secured and ready for any contingency."

"Graham, are you on board with all of this? I know some of it's new to you, but on a signal, everyone's got his job. And you guys know yours, I hear."

"Yes, we're all on board. My crew seemed to find their place and fit in right away," Graham said.

"Glad to hear it. Dutch told me how Bang took over archery training. I would love to have seen that." Dalton began to laugh and had to hold onto his shoulder when the laughter caused him pain. They all broke into much-needed chuckles.

"If he wasn't such a modest little guy, it wouldn't have been so damn comical, but he's so tiny; I just couldn't believe it. These kids certainly pull their own weight in the defense department," Dutch said.

"Yeah." Graham agreed. "Bang came to me like that. His mother had taught him well. She was amazing; kept herself alive long enough to hand him off to me. She waited until my father died; she watched me. I don't know how she did it, frankly. Her name was Hyun-Ok. I'll never forget her look of resolute courage." Graham looked up at Clarisse, who smiled at him.

"Never underestimate a mother's love," she said.

"She could have taken his life. Many did that," Dalton said.

"That's not an option for some mothers," Clarisse said, and Dalton saw her smile at Tala, who sat next to Graham with her hand on her swollen belly. They all knew what Clarisse meant; nothing else needed saying.

"It wasn't an option for her. That kid has saved my ass, and fed me more than once," Graham admitted. Dalton could tell with an ache in his heart for his own sons how Graham felt for the boy. Bang was as much Graham's own son as Hunter and Kade were Dalton's.

"Okay, well. I'm hoping to get out of this damn bed by tomorrow—if Doc here clears me, that is," Dalton said, smiling up at Clarisse.

She looked at him and affirmed his hopes. "I think that's possible, but you have to take it easy. These things take time. Your strength won't be back to one hundred percent for weeks."

"We may not have that much time. Any questions? No? Hey, Rick, do you have operators for the reapers?" Dalton said.

"Actually, yes. You'll be surprised who aced the test, but yes. We have five operators ready to go."

"All right, I'll see you guys in the morning. Stay vigilant," he said to dismiss everyone, and they filtered out of the room. Then Dalton turned to McCann and said, "Hey, can you hang here for a second?"

"Sure."

"Can't thank you enough. Sam told me what went down . . . what he saw from his perspective. That goddamned bear just wouldn't quit. Last thing I remember, I was pulling out my pistol and seeing the bear turn on someone else, but it wasn't one of us. I fired on the bear, not realizing it was attacking the enemy. What the hell happened? That's where I blacked out."

McCann swallowed his guilt over Steven's death before he could speak. "Nothing we did to distract the bear did a damn thing. I don't know how many shots we pumped into him before those frigging bastards showed up. They were firing on us. There was a bear attacking you. It was messed up," McCann said.

"That, my friend, is what we call a clusterfuck," Dalton explained.

McCann let out a sad chuckle. "Yeah, it was all that. Everyone was shooting, and I hit a big rock with the back of my boot against the brick wall and Steven was in front of me. Everything slowed down all of a sudden; I looked at the chaos and saw you trying to stab the bear, and you were sliding down the wall. I stopped shooting, picked up the rock, and jumped out of cover of the brick wall and launched it as hard as I could at the bear's head. Steven jumped in front of me because I was completely exposed, and . . . he recoiled backward over me. I knew what happened immediately." He looked down, shaking his head as he remembered the nightmare. "It's my fault he died. He was trying to cover me. I screwed up and he died. I should have warned him to him."

Dalton waited a moment for McCann's angst to die down. "McCann, in a clusterfuck, there is no time to explain. I've been there, when time slows down and you know whatever decision you make in the next split second will set off a chain reaction. No one but you blames you for Steven's death. It was *those* fuckers, and believe me, redemption is coming. You saved my life, man. You saved my sons from being completely orphaned. I owe you." Dalton shook McCann's hand.

"Thanks, Dalton. All the same, can Rick or someone else show me the hand signals you guys use so I can at least know how to communicate if this ever happens again?"

"Sure," Dalton said. "Ask Rick. I'm sure he'll show you. Hell, Sam taught us different hand signals and I think we use a combination of the two now, but honestly, from what Sam described, it probably wouldn't have made a difference."

Clarisse came back into the room, and both men turned to look at her. "Visiting time is over, guys. Dalton needs to sleep now," she said, and McCann headed for the door.

"Hey, McCann. Swing by tomorrow. I need to look at that arm again," Clarisse said as the young man waved and disappeared from sight.

"You are so mean," Dalton teased.

"You're tired. I can tell," Clarisse said as she readied a shot full of fluid and inserted it into Dalton's IV tube.

"Hey, what the hell was that?" he said and grabbed her around the thigh. "Don't put me to sleep now."

"You are such a baby, and a terrible patient."

"I seem to remember you being quite a naughty doctor recently," Dalton said, pulling her down to lip level.

Graham grabbed his tray and followed Mark through the dinner line. "You're on watch tonight?" he asked Mark as Olivia spooned the game catch of the day's casserole onto his plate. "Thank you," he said, grabbing a pan and tearing it away from the rest in the row. He was starving, and the smell of rolls rising all day had left him weak and salivating, even if they weren't Tala's famous rolls.

"Yeah, McCann and I," Mark answered. "Rick said I couldn't take watch with Marcy. She's too distracting for me, he says." Mark stuffed a roll into his mouth, then grabbed another.

"Is that where the girls are now?" Graham asked.

"Yeah, both she and Macy are on watch. Rick had them shoot and cleared them both for guard duty this afternoon while you were on duty."

"Great. So, I'll be relieving you after your shift tonight." Graham found the table Tala had chosen and sat down beside her.

"Graham, why did you tell Rick I couldn't take a shift on guard duty?" Tala asked. She was angry, and her eyes turned black as coal when she was mad at him. Graham looked at Mark, who'd heard the remark and suddenly became enthralled with his own meal.

"I'd think the answer was obvious," Graham said.

"I can still shoot, Graham. You should have asked me. Or we should have talked about this before you made the decision for me. You know I don't like that. I'm pregnant, not useless," Tala said.

"Can we talk about this later? In the tent, maybe?" Graham kissed her on the head and touched the small of her back, pulling her against him on the bench. He hugged her, knowing all of this was new and different and she felt out of place.

Tala waited a moment and then leaned close to his ear. "I'm not sure you're going to be in the tent with me tonight," she whispered with a smirk.

"Yes I will, Tala. You're not getting out of my sight. I'm trying to protect you and our child. You're a powerful, amazing woman, but hell, I couldn't live without you. It would kill me, and our baby is preciously close to life. No, Tala. I won't let you do guard duty. You can be mad at me, but I'm doing it out of love."

She leaned into Graham, resting her head on his chest. Pouting, she said, "I'm not mad. I'm scared and hormonal. I'm frustrated, and even *your* shirts aren't even big enough to cover me now."

He smiled into her hair. "You're beautiful, Tala. My God, I think you're even sexier now than ever, swollen with our child growing inside of you. It nearly killed me to leave you alone this morning." Graham knew from experience that once he started talking like this into her ear, she would turn shades of red in front of everyone else.

Tala knew it too. "Stop, Graham, please. Not now." She leaned into him again and whispered with a wicked smile, "Later, maybe."

The Malefic Nation seeped through spring rains and slithered on their bellies in the mud, hidden by the early fog of day and the dark blanket of night. A few pathfinders at first, then legions of them. First a trickle, and then a steady murky stream, growing ever larger, lying in wait and watching.

Graham leaned back in the guard shack against the wall of the quarantine building. He blinked carefully, still not used to the night vision contacts. *I can't believe I let them talk me into this.* He'd heard about these things, but didn't think he'd ever find himself wearing them; knowing his eyes glowed green like a cyborg was unsettling.

Rick had assured him that these were better than night vision goggles, or NVGs, which were plagued with depth perception issues. He had recounted the time they'd descended out of a Nighthawk helicopter in Iraq when the approaching ground suddenly appeared to leap forward. Rick had landed hard and knocked himself out, wrenching his ankle in the process due to the damn thing; *items may be closer than they appear.* He then walked painfully for two days with his ankle wrapped in duct tape.

Graham and Sam had both opted for the contacts, a neat little tech invention that Rick was proud to have gotten his hands on before the world fell apart. They were even rumored to have been used in the Bin Laden raid back before all of this started. Rick explained that the recent discovery of graphene, an ultralight, strong carbon only one atom thick, made it all possible.

What bothered Graham at the moment was the gel magnet that powered the thing; you adhered it to your eyelid, and the weight of it took some getting used to; with each blink there was an extra thickness. Graham figured that in time he would get used to the feeling, but for now it distracted him every time he creased his eyelid.

He scanned the area in front of him from left to right and met Sam's green glowing eyes peering back at him from the far right. It

209

was an eerie sensation. He blinked again and peered to the west, scanning up and down the dark forest for anything unusual. With only starlight to shine through the night, the iridescent green shone bright. Had the moonlight drenched the forest, he thought it'd be bright as summer high noon through the scope, and he'd need sunglasses to get by without his eyes watering.

The earpiece clicked once and Graham spoke softly into the microphone clipped to his collar. "Clear. Rain's picking up. Over."

"Reuben's relieving you in ten. Over." Rick said.

"Copy," Graham said back. The microphone remained open in case there was any feedback, or to save a panicked step if one became necessary.

Graham's ear went silent once again, and the rain pattered softly against the lush leaves and long, desiccated needles covering the ground between the trees. He found his mind drifting to Tala, lying warm and swollen in their tent, and how he might put it gently to McCann to take Bang into his own tent for a night without revealing his amorous intentions. *Maybe insomnia,* he thought. *Yeah, that would work. The boy snores anyway.* He could claim for one night that Bang's snoring was keeping him up. *It might work.*

Suddenly his brain showed him an outline that shouldn't be there. Graham thought it might be a trick of his imagination. He stared at the anomaly a millisecond longer, making sure it wasn't his mind trying to make false logical sense of loose elements. But the more he stared, he couldn't deny that there was someone there. He was out in the open, and the image knew he was there too, with glowing green eyes staring back at him. The hair on Graham's neck started a slow procession toward saluting.

Without moving at all, he whispered into his microphone, "Rick, ten-fourteen."

A moment passed while Graham observed the figure for any movement. Then he heard a confused breath over his earpiece, "What the hell's a ten-fourteen, Graham?"

Graham suddenly realized he was using Ennis's police code rules instead of the agreed-upon military radio code, but his mind just couldn't recall what the hell the right response that was at this crucial moment.

"Talk to me, Graham. What the hell do you mean? Is someone there?" Rick asked him.

"Uh-huh," he said softly.

"How many?"

"One, so far."

"Where?"

"Northwest. Barely see him," Graham said slowly, hoping his voice wouldn't carry in what little wind there was.

"Don't engage. We're coming," Rick advised.

"Yep, not engaging," Graham responded, now observing the solid outline of a man. Then he saw what looked like a leg draped in a sheet move forward and, instead of crouching down, the man came sat on the ground. The glowing figure suddenly aimed something in his direction.

"Ah shit, he's moving!"

"Down, Graham!" Rick yelled right behind him after catching sight of the guy aiming at Graham's position. Sam suddenly began firing from a separate position, and then all hell broke loose.

Light streaks came at Graham, and what sounded like bullets whizzed by his head as he dropped to the ground. Something hit his chest and, for a second, Graham didn't remember the vest he wore. The impact robbed him of his breath momentarily. Suddenly several more figures moved in the neon-green distance—those he hadn't detected. What formerly looked like brush and twigs now morphed into human forms, their bodies draped in cloth.

Graham heard a scream coming from the depth of green, and a figure emerged, clutching a spear that was embedded in his chest. Another man yanked one from his thigh.

"Reapers!" yelled Dalton's voice in Graham's ear.

"Copy," Reuben answered.

Graham aimed his rifle and looked through the scope at one of the increasing number of assailants, firing bright bursts of gunfire in his direction. He eased the nose of his rifle through an opening in the railing of the guard post while crouching on his belly. He fired three rapid bursts and the figure fell, only to be replaced by another.

They were coming now, more and more of them through the woods. The first mysterious figures were now replaced by a wall of men in sheets blasting tiny lights at them. When one went down, two more could be seen in the distance.

"Reapers ready," Rick said through the earpiece.

Graham continued to fire from his concealed position and watched as a few fell, while others recoiled and continued on, blasting back at his position. He knew he'd have to move soon or he'd meet the same demise as his first kill.

"Ready." Tala's voice caught his attention.

He was nauseated now, knowing she had a lethal job to do, but he kept on firing. He knew the five reaper operators were Rick, Tala, Clarisse, Lucy, and McCann. Knowing Tala was safe but stressed operating one of the killing machines drove Graham nuts, but he couldn't worry about that now.

He also knew Reuben, Mark, and the twins were hauling the rest of the camp's occupants away and setting in motion their evacuation plan as the action unfolded.

He sighted another figure, and sent three short bursts to the guy's chest causing him to fall. Aiming again to the left, he heard the reapers begin, and the chatter in his ear increased suddenly. He picked out a few frustrated huffs and expletives, and Dalton told the group to try and remain silent to keep the line open for commands. A few more four-letter words seeped through, but Graham didn't have the time to focus on the voices, with machine gun fire coming from the reapers and the shrill screams of the surprised invaders.

Another bullet whizzed by his head and he felt a hand grab his jeans on the back of his thigh and yank him backward. Graham shot a glance backward. It was Dutch.

"Behind me!" Dutch yelled. Graham didn't need to be told twice, and hustled behind the bigger man, both of them taking cover behind the quarantine building.

"Keep shooting!" Dutch yelled.

"I am! But they just keep coming!"

"The reapers will take out more of them soon. Don't get discouraged. Keep going! Dalton will let us know if we need to fall back."

Graham aimed again and fired. There was no lack of targets available. Sam fired repeatedly from his position to the east. He doubted the reapers would make a dent in this crowd. He could see that they were outnumbered; he only hoped they weren't outgunned.

Each person knew his or her position and responsibility. And each knew that, above all else, this wouldn't be easy. What Graham didn't expect was the sheer number of enemy soldiers descending upon their location.

Dalton kept his eyes on the screens and the five reaper operators at the same time. They all sat or stood wherever they felt most comfortable. His main priority was to keep them safe as they battled the enemy less than six hundred feet from their position. If the enemy gained on them, he'd hustle them out of there fast.

With night vision goggles over their eyes, they adapted to each camera and the controllers in their hands. Dalton watched each move, toggle, and fire his or her assigned reaper. In doing so, he kept track of each operator's progress through his own video feed. Five tree-affixed machine guns made a hell of a racket, and in an instant Dalton was back in the bedlam of Afghanistan.

He sat in his chair with one eye on the operators and the other on the monitors.

"One, go left. Don't let them flank," he said.

"I'm . . . trying," McCann said.

"You've got a hundred rounds each. Make them count," Dalton reminded them, spinning back to the monitors. They had no way of knowing how many there were. A Humvee appeared in the background as several assailants rushed for cover behind it when reaper number 3, Tala, yelled, "You goddamn cowards, come back here!"

"That's right, Tala, keep after them!" Dalton cried. "Remember, this isn't a video game. This is for real. Their guns are real, and if we let them through, we're in trouble."

Rick held his position on the right flank, but their numbers were increasing. A thicket of trees held cover for several, and the rapid fire of the number 1 gun rarely ceased.

"Talk to me, Rick," Dalton said.

"Can't. Busy now," Rick said, his attention fully fixated on the killing task at hand. He was sweating, and Dalton began to worry that his friend wouldn't be able to keep them back.

Seven to ten jihadists slipped past Rick's reaper using their comrades for shields. "You fuckers!" Rick yelled, turning his reaper in their direction, heading right for Sam's position.

"Sam! Take cover!" Dalton warned.

Rick shot down the first three, only to have the last two do the same thing others had done before, using the dead bodies of their brothers to shield themselves before they slipped behind the trees.

"Sam, you're up. Three o'clock," Dalton advised.

"Copy," Sam said.

Rick had returned to his position, taking down as many as he could. He had slightly less than half of his hundred tracer bullets left to go when they showed how bad his aim was and revealed that the reaper was about to shake itself apart completely from the rapid-fire invasion. He continued to expel as many lethal shots as possible to make up for the numbers and account for the recoil, but at some point reaper number 5 ceased to work at all. "Fuck it," Rick said, pulling it off.

"Number 4, hand yours to Rick," Dalton said.

Dalton knew Clarisse had no problem tossing her controller over to Rick; she was capable of doing this work, but she was needed elsewhere. She pulled off her NVGs, and the dim light of the media tent momentarily blinded her. She blinked several times, and Dalton tipped his chin over to McCann. He'd noticed a blossoming bloodstain on the young man's shirt, but there was no time to deal with examining a wound now. The tension in the tent could not be more profound.

"Clarisse, be a runner. I need to know how far Reuben is on the evac," Dalton said.

She turned and left right away while the chaos outside continued.

"Sam, status," Dalton asked.

"Oh, they're done. Working up with the ceased number 5. They're starting to come through there. I can do this all day, but I only have so much ammo, Dalton."

"Graham?" Dalton asked.

"There are too many of them," Graham said.

Then an explosion rocked the ground. The four remaining Reaper controllers all braced their footing.

"What the hell was that? Report!" Dalton yelled.

"Fucking mortar!" Dutch yelled over the din of war. "On fire, too. Pull back!"

"Incoming!" Graham broke in, shouting. The ground rocked again.

"Graham!" Tala yelled. "Graham!" She whipped off her NVGs and ran for the door. Dalton caught her just in time for yet another mortar round impact. He covered her body as she fell to the ground.

"Fall back!" Dalton ordered as Clarisse arrived and helped Dalton and Tala up. Reuben appeared with their own Humvee, and Rick pushed all the operators out of the burning tent and into the vehicle.

"McCann, go with Rick. Retrieve the others!" Dalton ordered.

Tala cried, and Clarisse held her. "Come on, Dalton," Clarisse implored him.

Dalton cut his eyes away from her and closed the door. Pounding the metal twice, he nodded to Reuben, who floored it. Clarisse's scream faded with his name as he turned toward the fire.

Dalton's silhouette stood out against the flames as he pulled out his pistol with one hand and a long knife with the other.

"Tala!" Clarisse yelled, holding the sobbing woman by the shoulders and shaking her to get her attention as Reuben raced away. Then she whispered, "I'm going back. Give me your gun and extra magazines. If we don't return, take care of Addy and the boys for me."

Tears streamed down Tala cheeks. She glanced quickly at the back of Reuben's head and nodded, handing Clarisse her pistol. Lucy handed over hers, as well as the NVGs she happened to have with her. "Get them back," Tala said.

"I will," she said and hugged them both briefly. Then she slyly smiled. She opened her jacket, pulled it down past her shoulders, and tucked her glasses into the inside pocket, and strapped the NVGs to her belt loop. She holstered one of the extra pistols to her thigh and slid the other into the waist of her cargo pants, placing the extra magazines into a leg pocket. She zipped up her jacket and pulled the hood over her head, cinching the straps tightly around her face.

"Reuben!" she commanded, alarmingly loud and clear. She swung open the door of the Humvee and leaned backward, ready to roll for his view. She didn't give him a chance to make a decision. As soon as he saw what Clarisse was about to do, Reuben automatically began to brake. She glanced quickly at Tala and Lucy one last time, then dove out of the vehicle with her arms protecting her head, spinning with momentum upon the ground. She knelt up on one knee and watched as the Humvee picked up speed again and gained distance.

Clarisse assessed herself quickly for injuries. Detecting no major pain, she pulled her own pistol out of her side holster, checked a magazine, and loaded it into the chamber. She holstered it again, donned the NVGs, and ran into the forest to gain cover and cut through the woods toward the gunshots and the growing blaze. The closer she got, the more her vision began to fail. The NVGs were too bright and her eyes watered, so she tore them off and secured them to her belt loop.

It was time. She'd been trained along with all the others in tactical maneuvers, and it was time to tap that training. Shadows passed before the blaze. Many were wearing traditional wear. Some wore commando gear. Her mission was to locate the guys and get them the hell out of there. She knew Dalton wouldn't last long—especially not in his condition.

A shadow passed too close to her, and Clarisse dove for cover behind a tree. The barracks were now fully ablaze; the enemy were torching everything and beginning to overrun the camp. There had to have been at least a hundred of them when all this started. Then a red pinpoint of light shone on her thigh; she panicked and braced for the shot. It blinked, and she followed the light. It was Sam; he was signaling her. Hiding in a tree, he motioned for her to come to him.

Clarisse ran toward Sam as an assailant yelled something in a foreign language. She felt a shot land near her feet. With her right arm extended and her weapon drawn, she hit him twice in the chest, not three feet away. Sam finished him off with a shot to the head as she joined him in the tree.

"Where are they?"

"Dalton's fine," Sam said.

"Where is he?"

"Right flank. He's getting Dutch," Sam said.

"And McCann?"

"He's with Rick, getting Graham."

That's when she saw the blood as the fire reflected light on Sam's arm. His hands were covered in it.

"Where are you hit?" she gasped.

"Thigh," Sam said. She felt his leg, and her hand came away warm and slick. She peeled off her jacket, pulled up her thin cotton T-shirt, and ripped the hemline around it off, pulling it over her head. She stretched the loop of fabric, then tied it around Sam's leg to stem the flow of blood long enough to keep him conscious.

He grabbed her by the shoulder and growled at her, "Get out of here, Clarisse!"

"Shut up!" Clarisse barked back. "Stay awake, Sam. I'll find them and send them here to meet you."

"No," he said and grabbed her by the sleeve. "They'll capture you. Don't you understand what they're doing?"

She yanked herself free. "Stay awake, Sam. I'll be right back." She put her jacket back on over her bloodstained shirt and leaped forward. She'd go for Dalton first. She had to. Taking advantage of the forest, she slunk from tree cover to the dark shadows, ducking in and out of the ravenous light of the blazing camp.

She aimed farther to the right flank, staying in the shadows and springing from one patch of darkness to another. Each step brought her closer to her own demise, but she went there willingly. To kill them if she could. She wanted to kill them. To murder, maim, and annihilate those whose own selfishness had destroyed not only a nation but also humanity itself.

With gun drawn, Clarisse headed toward the increasing gunfire to the right of the camp. At the next rise, around the former mess hall, she came across a dead assailant who she assumed had succumbed to Dalton's handiwork and retrieved his automatic rifle a few feet away. Slinging the weapon over her back by its strap, she ran on toward the action.

Two aggressors came around the corner, and she shot the first one in the head at point-blank range with her right hand drawn across her body. She calculated, with swift reasoning, that she had a split second to hit the other one. With the left hand she retrieved the second pistol at her waistband, crossed it under her right arm, and blasted the other guy in the stomach. Then she brought her right arm around to finish him off with a headshot before he came within five feet of her. Without missing a step Clarisse ran on, weapons in both hands. She moved closer to the sounds of war and of murder, knowing she might find one or all of her friends dead by now. She had to recover them. She at least had to try.

"Nooo!"

Clarisse stopped in her tracks. It was Dalton's agonized voice, followed by a barrage of gunfire more intense than before. She continued toward his location, terrified of what she might find.

She could no longer even register the sounds of battle—they were too intense—and came around the right end of the guard shack to see Dalton, kneeling behind a Jeep so riddled with bullets that before long the shield it provided would became a trap.

Dalton fired on a group to the left of his position. Clarisse searched for Dutch, but he was nowhere in sight. Five men fired at Dalton while another loaded what looked to Clarisse like a rocket launcher. She aimed for that one. She had to buy some time to run in the open to Dalton, twenty yards away, and get him the hell out of there. She wasn't certain he could stand by the way he knelt against the Jeep. She couldn't waste any more time; she had to get him out now.

Clarisse holstered the pistols and pulled the newly acquired rifle around to her chest. She checked the load, shoved the stock into her shoulder, and aimed the rifle at the man with the rocket launcher, following the line of his arm to directly target the rocket launcher's ordnance. The shot she fired exploded the round within the chamber, killing the operator and two others standing nearby with a great blast. It was enough of a diversion to run the twenty yards in the open to get to Dalton's position, and Clarisse ran before she had a split second to convince herself otherwise.

Dalton stared at the explosion in surprise and then turned behind him as Clarisse barreled toward him. She'd rearmed her right hand with the pistol along the way and fired again at an attacker dressed in white who was aiming at her. Dalton turned his attention to the same assailant, and as the white-robed man went down Clarisse slid into Dalton's side.

"Clarisse!" Dalton yelled in horror and dismay, and he pushed her down. It barely registered that Dalton was uttering curse words at her; his lips moved, but Clarisse heard nothing. She turned, scanned the enemy, and pinpointed what she was looking for: their magazines. She wanted to light them up; this picking off one at time was taking too long.

Where the ordnance for one rocket launcher was located there was sure to be more. With the fire lighting their position, Clarisse aimed again and fired on the back of a vehicle she suspected carried their cache. Once Dalton realized what she aimed for, he gave up trying to chastise her and he fired repeatedly until they were both suddenly taking cover from the flash explosion generated by a lucky shot.

Clarisse pulled Dalton to his feet, looping his right arm over her shoulder, and they both ran, covering one another from the volley of incoming shots. Clarisse dragged them toward one of their own Jeeps as Dalton began to lose consciousness; leaning against the door, he began to slide down it. Clarisse imagined that, in his condition, he was blacking out after the massive adrenaline rush.

"Get in!" she screamed and opened the door, pushing and shoving him into the seat.

"Get out of here, Clarisse!" he yelled. "They've got Dutch." That was the last thing he uttered before passing out altogether.

Clarisse threw the Jeep in drive and sped west through their former haven, now nearly burned to the ground. She drove madly,

---

hoping to find the others before the entire camp was overrun. Shots pinged off the Jeep when it became visible between shadows.

They saw her before she saw them; she nearly ran right into them. They came out of the shadows directly in front of her—only two stood—and Clarisse slammed the Jeep to a stop. She recognized Graham, who had another man in a fireman's carry over his back. He and McCann rushed around to the back of the Jeep, tossed Rick's body inside, and jumped in themselves. Still the enemy shot at them. Graham remained on the tailgate, returning fire.

Clarisse glanced in the rearview mirror, catching McCann's face in the firelight, his expression one of having witnessed hell. In slow motion, he pounded on the metal and screamed, "Go, go!" Clarisse stomped on the gas, and the Jeep sped away into the shadow of darkness.

The enemy were chanting now, raising their rifles high overhead and dancing in the firelight. The scene reminded her of jackals, in celebration over a kill. These people were long past human. Now Dutch was among them; they were leaving him to his death. The thought ate at Clarisse, but they had no choice. Not now.

She stopped near the woods where she had left Sam, and pointed toward his location, yelling, "Get Sam!" As Graham ran to the woods, Sam appeared, leaning against a tree. Graham retrieved him while Clarisse checked her rearview mirror.

They were still coming; she saw the movement of two motorcycles trailing them against the light. Then she heard a shot hit the Jeep. "Hurry!" McCann yelled as he returned fire, trying to hold them back.

Graham struggled to get Sam closer, and Clarisse threw the Jeep in reverse to block their position from incoming fire. Everyone screamed at Graham to hurry, and one of the motorcycles pulled in front of them. Just as Graham and Sam were seated, the rider aimed directly at Clarisse. She floored it, and his body slammed onto the hood, and then the windshield, shattering it, but she kept going. She couldn't see a thing and shoved her fist through the glass to get a better view. The guy was either dead or stunned; if he wasn't dead, he would be soon enough.

McCann continued to shoot at the other rider, and Clarisse assumed he got him when the firing ceased. She raced onward.

"Are we clear?" she yelled.

"I don't know!" McCann yelled.

"Keep looking," Graham said more calmly, climbing into the front seat over Dalton's unconscious form and opening the hatch of the Jeep's sunroof. He pulled his pistol out and pushed himself waist high through the opening.

"Be careful!" Clarisse said, then turned to Sam. "You okay?"

"I'm fine," Sam said weakly.

"Stay awake, Sam," she implored him.

Graham leaned over to grab the body of the guy on the hood of the Jeep; amid the sound of scraping glass, the body slid from the hood and onto the side of the road. Graham came back inside and said, "He was way dead."

"Good," Clarisse answered.

"Where are we going?" Graham asked. "We can't lead them to the others."

"No. I agree. We'll find a place. We have a cache west of here," she said.

"How's Dalton?" Graham asked, trying to feel for his pulse.

"He'll be fine." She had to ask but was afraid of the answer. "And Rick?"

"He's got a pulse. He was hit in the head during one of the mortar rounds," McCann said.

Graham put his hand on Clarisse's shoulder. "Why don't you pull over. Let me drive now."

"No. I know where we're going. We're almost there," she said. She knew that Graham was trying to comfort her, afraid she'd break down soon. What he didn't know was that she was far ahead of him now. She wasn't too concerned about Rick, Sam, or even Dalton's condition. She'd make sure they'd be fine in time. Right now she was thinking about one of their own, and the cache of equipment she was about to have access to, and plotting. She had to get back to Dutch before the sun rose.

Reuben pulled into the clearing, unfolded the map, and used a penlight to check their location. Lucy leaned forward from the backseat, with Tala next to her. "Are we lost?" she asked.

He glanced back at her soft green eyes and her pale skin, which nearly glowed in the dark. He'd hardly said a word to the occupants in the backseat after their escape. He'd shut them out completely as he raced toward safety. The enemy had been ruthless, Clarisse was probably dead, and Dalton would blame him for that. That is, if any of them made it out of there alive; Reuben had his doubts. He saw the other prepper vehicles in the rearview mirror. There were too many of them, no matter what tricks they had up their sleeves.

"No. We're not lost. I'm waiting for the signal."

"Oh," Lucy said and then asked, "Where are the dogs?"

"They were in the first load. We thought it was best to keep them with the children as an added measure of defense."

Suddenly three flashes of blue light caught Lucy's attention, ahead of them in the dark.

"Is that the signal?" she asked.

"Yes. That's it." Reuben put the truck in drive and headed out of the clearing, into the forest, while Mark moved brush out of the way for him.

The realization that he would have to relay bad news became more daunting the farther Reuben went. The plan had gone off without a hitch until Dalton had decided to play commando. Now Reuben was the senior in command until the others showed up . . . if they showed up at all. Leading this group was a huge responsibility, and he wasn't confident he was up for the task.

So far it looked as if Mark was acting according to the plan, which was a good sign. He rolled down the window, and Mark stepped onto the running panel and held on. "Go ahead. The path winds to the right," Mark whispered.

"Who else is on watch?"

"Macy has the front. Don't worry; no one's getting past her. And no one could get past Lawoaka either, without me tagging along," Mark said.

"Ah." Reuben understood now; His own daughter had wicked sharp sight and no sense of humor. It had worried him, the way these kids were growing up. They were trained daily to defend and kill. They'd kill or be killed from now on to survive. He wasn't sure he wanted this for them. Perhaps death was more just, more humane. He hadn't made up his mind yet, but the question nagged at his soul.

He stopped in front of a weathered, gray one-story hunting lodge. Mark opened the back door for Lucy and Tala.

"You made it," Mark said, embracing Tala.

"Hi, Mark. Is everyone okay?" Tala asked.

"Yeah, we're fine. Where are Graham and McCann?"

She looked to Reuben, then said, "There was some difficulty getting out. We think they're on their way, but we haven't heard yet."

"Nothing came over the radio?" Reuben asked him.

"We haven't set anything up. No tracers, right?" Mark said.

"That was a trick question. Yes, you're right. They either show up or they don't," Reuben answered.

Marcy emerged to usher Lucy and Tala inside a dimly lit cabin.

"You guys run into any trouble on your way here? Any locals?" Reuben asked Mark as they walked back to the entrance.

"Not a soul," Mark said as Sheriff ran up to his side in the dark.

"Hey, buddy. You keeping these guys in line?" Reuben said as Sheriff sniffed him.

"Yeah, Sheriff's been on edge since we got here. We hear wolf cries every now and then. We're sure there are no other people nearby this location?" Mark asked.

Reuben surveyed the area—as much as he could see in the moonlight. "We're not sure of anything right now, son. I only remembered this place on a hunting trip I took ten years ago. I gave you three possible locations. This one was thankfully unoccupied. We'll wait a few days for the others to arrive, and decide if we move on or stay here," Reuben said.

"It's fine for now. The house is at least big enough, and defendable," Mark said. And there it was again for Reuben: this seventeen-year-old kid was worried about defense. He wasn't studying for his SAT test, he wasn't working on his favorite ride. It was life and death he worried about. His survival instincts had already taken over. Is this how humankind was meant to continue?

Suddenly, a hand touched Reuben on the back and he nearly pulled his weapon around. "Jesus! Don't do that!" he warned Macy.

"Hi, Reuben," she said, hugging him.

"Seriously, you could get yourself killed sneaking up like that," he said.

"You'd never shoot me," she said, smiling.

"Only for your own good," he said.

Macy raised an eyebrow at him, but then shrugged it off. "Where are the others? They were supposed to be with you."

"There was some trouble. They should be here soon."

"It'll be light in another hour," she said.

"We'll wait for them," Mark said, "as long as it takes."

"Who are your people?"

"Americans!" Dutch yelled in angry protest. It was the only answer he would utter.

He smiled in defiance at the enemy behind bloodied, split lips and a nose he knew was broken. He was having some trouble breathing, but remained silent as he knelt down before them with his arms tied behind his back. The man holding him around the neck shoved Dutch forward, causing him to fall face forward into the ground.

"Tell us how many there are!"

They would torture him first. He knew the drill. He'd seen it time and time again. Hell, most Americans had no idea how they tortured their prisoners before they beheaded them; it didn't matter if they were men, women, or children.

They were animals, and took pleasure in their savagery. With nothing more than an alpha dominance mentality, they perceived their prisoners' submission as their right, and any act they could come up with—no matter how vile—they would undertake, repeatedly, to achieve that submission.

I'm dead. It's only a matter of minutes now, Dutch thought.

They'd already hung him from a tree for a time by his hands. His shoulders had sustained his entire body's weight, and they felt as if they would come out of their sockets at any time. They beat him with sticks while yelling questions at him. When that didn't work, they dropped him to the ground, where he remained.

Dutch tried to block out the tremendous pain and kept his thoughts on Lucy, knowing she would survive. His prosthesis was nowhere in sight; he didn't remember when they took it off of him.

A boot landed on the back of his left elbow. They jerked him up against the pressure and repeated again, "How many? Special forces?"

Nothing. He would give them absolutely nothing except to tell them that they hadn't won. "Americans," was all he would say. Knowing that he had saved Lucy from this hell would bring him peace in his last fleeting breath.

The butt end of his captor's rifle hit Dutch in the jaw. They were done with him for now. He fell down again, face first into the ground, and lay there until the lights dimmed.

Clarisse pulled up near the hidden bunker.

"This is it?" Graham asked.

"Yeah." She pointed toward a tree grove. "There's a metal bunker with a cache of equipment there behind the trees. Let me open the door, and we'll get these guys inside. We spent many weekends setting these up in various locations. We've got med supplies in here, and enough room for all of us—for now." She and Graham ran for the trees and moved brush out of the way. "The keypad is here somewhere," Clarisse said, searching the exterior.

"Here it is," Graham said, pulling up on the locking device. Clarisse typed in a code and the latch opened easily. She scanned the night sky, trying to predict how much time they had before daylight. Graham met her eyes.

"I'm going back with you," he said. She had no idea he would guess her intentions.

"No, I can do it alone," she said

"No you can't. Not this. If there's a way, we can do it together," Graham said, and Clarisse had to admit he was right.

"Let's get them inside and load up." She swung up the metal gate to the bunker.

"There's a light on the right there," she told Graham, and when he hit switch a fluorescent glow started out dim, but quickly increased.

"Hurry. We need to keep this door closed."

McCann was already bringing Sam in; he was bloody, with one arm draped over McCann's shoulder.

"Bring him here," Clarisse said, not believing her eyes. There was so much blood. She hurried into the eight-by-ten bunker, pulling out a cot and setting it up for Sam to lie on. McCann began to arrange two more cots while she pulled medical equipment off the shelves.

Each bunker had been set up the same, with weapons, food, and medical equipment for future needs.

"McCann, I need your help with the others," Graham called out.

Clarisse knelt down at Sam's side. He was pale and barely conscious, glassy-eyed. She checked his wound and ripped open his pant leg to discover that his femoral vein was nicked. He'd be dead if much more time had elapsed, but at least it was repairable. She left the tourniquet on for now and set up an IV.

She smiled at him. "You're gonna be fine, Sam."

"I know it. It's not my time yet." He grabbed Clarisse's arm, adding, "It's not yours either, and I know you're thinking of going back. Dutch knows he's a dead man. You can't save him, so please don't try."

"I'm putting you to sleep now, Sam. Don't worry, my friend. I still have a few tricks up my sleeve."

"Not enough, Clarisse. Not enough for this," Sam said before sliding into a deep sleep.

She worked quickly. She disinfected herself and his leg as fast as possible and then McCann opened the sterile surgical kit for her.

"You have to handle this now, she said to McCann. "We won't be gone too long. If we don't return by sundown, get them into the truck and go to the planned location. I'm sorry I have to leave this to you," she said, feeling guilty about the immense responsibility she was placing on the young man. She looked up at McCann, who watched her scalpel technique. As usual, he had a toothpick in his mouth; Clarisse had no idea where he kept those things, but he seemed to have an endless supply of them.

"I've got it covered, Clarisse," McCann said. "Don't worry. Dalton just needs to sleep it off. He's fine. Rick, I don't know. His vitals are fine, but it's a head injury, and he'll come out of it or he won't. Sam here nearly bled to death, but he'll be okay now with this repair."

"Good. Okay, there are MREs in here and more medical supplies and lots of ammo. Read the labels. Keep the door closed and locked. *Do not* use the radio. Try to sleep if you can, and we should be back before noon, no matter what."

"Don't worry about us; get Dutch back if you can."

At least I have his support, Clarisse thought, then turned to face McCann. "Okay, he's all set now. You can close the wound yourself. I'll clean up, and we can get going," she said, turning to Graham.

"I'll load up a few things," Graham said, and he began pulling supplies from the shelves he thought might come in handy.

"Make sure you add *that* one." She pointed to a rectangular, army-green bundle. "And plenty of *those*, too."

Graham raised his eyebrows at her.

"We're not going back empty-handed."

In her sleeveless shirt, Clarisse drenched both arms with saline again to wash off the blood that seeped past her glove line. The water was cold, and the sound of the splashing seemed foreign to her in this small, quiet room.

Three of the strongest men she'd ever known lay before her, helpless, on cots on the ground. The enemy had done this to them, and it might never end. They might have to run like this forever, until the last of them perished.

"I'm ready," Graham said. "Let's go."

Clarisse donned her bloodied jacket and knelt at Dalton's side before she left. She caressed his scarred face and kissed him gently.

"I love you, Dalton. Good-bye for now."

Graham had topped off the Jeep's gas tank before they left, and now they rode in silence. The sun was beginning to rise. Graham glanced briefly at Clarisse in the passenger seat. She was quiet in thought and far away; they both were, but now it was time to plot and plan.

"It's impossible. You know that, right?" he said.

He glanced at her again to see if she was ignoring him or simply contriving a possible rescue scenario.

She shook her head. "It's not impossible. They think we've left." Only the road noise interrupted the next few hushed moments.

"It's not fair," Clarisse said, referring to the glorious scarlet-hued sunrise forming in the east. "It shouldn't be so beautiful."

Graham stepped on the accelerator. They had to get into position. In his mind, there were only two possible outcomes, and both involved saving Dutch.

"If we set up above the ridge, we'll have plenty of cover. We can see them and they won't necessarily be able to see us—until we fire the rockets, that is. Then we'll have time to get out of there pretty quick," he said.

"Or, make sure there's no one left to come after us," she answered. They both knew this mission might mean their death sentence.

"They can't be allowed to track us back," Graham said.

"Even if we get them all, they'll send others. They'll come for us again. They won't stop. We have to find a way to wipe the trail clean," Clarisse said.

Graham could only nod, though he had no idea how they'd manage that.

Trees flew past his window. He'd stop soon and they'd pack up their gear and start hiking through the forest the rest of the way to meet the ridge that overlooked the burned-out preppers' camp.

"Pull over here," Clarisse said before he'd made the decision himself.

Graham ran the Jeep off the road and pulled up to the tree line of the forest leading to camp. He then backed the Jeep into the forest cover, leaving them a quick getaway if need be.

"This'll be perfect," Graham said.

"Let's hope so. It's our only chance. Leave the keys in the ignition." seeing the questioning look on Graham's face, she added, "In case one of us doesn't make it back, we won't have to worry who has the keys."

Graham left the keys on the seat, wondering if he'd see them again. After opening the back of the Jeep, Clarisse removed her jacket, tied it around her waist, and began reloading ammo and packing every possible advantage into their clothing.

Graham slung a bag containing a rocket-propelled grenade launcher over his shoulder, then placed several rounds into Clarisse's backpack. "Don't fall," he suggested as an attempt at humor. Finally he grabbed Rick's rifle and all the ammo he could carry.

"Do you need your glasses?" he asked as Clarisse tightened her chestnut hair into a straight ponytail. He noticed goose bumps on her bare, sleeveless arms.

"No. I'm farsighted. And they were crushed when I bailed out of Reuben's Jeep, anyway." She laughed, not certain why she found that humorous.

Graham smiled. "Let's do this," he said, and with the sun fully up behind them they entered the relative darkness of the forest — come what may.

"Sun's up. What do you think?" Mark asked Reuben.

"We're settled for now until we hear something."

"Damn, I wish I'd stayed with them." Mark had just traded his position off with Marcy. They were all dragging from the stress of the last twenty-four hours—and especially the previous night's battle.

"I'm pretty sure Graham made the right decision where you're concerned. It was his call. You need to be here taking care of these people," Reuben reminded him.

They'd just met at the cabin, and while the others took watch Olivia met them at the door with MREs and said in a voice meant as a warning, "Eat, and then sleep." After that, she returned to the kids, changing it to a singsong, nothing-is-wrong voice. Reuben marveled at how she could do that so quickly. His own wife was on watch now, along with Lucy and Tala, and he had no idea how they could go on like this. Of course, that didn't matter right now. He was the lead, and he needed to keep everyone both positive and ready to roll in case they were being trailed. Not knowing the fate of the others weighed them all down.

"I don't know if I can eat," Mark said.

Reuben turned his MRE on the long side and tore it that way instead of the expected short end. "Like this," he said. "You fuel up, or you stop and they die," Reuben said, swinging his spork around toward the children playing in the main room. "Doesn't matter what the envelope is labeled. You eat it and drink clean water. Sleep when you're allowed, and get back up and do it again. Clear?"

"Got it," Mark said, emulating Reuben's side-tear tactic.

Reuben fished a heaping sporkful of some kind of cold tomato-based pasta and shoved it into his mouth, "Mmmm," he said as Mark drank more water. Soon their MRE packets were empty and both bedded down on the wood floor with their rolls along the wall in the communal whoever-needs-to-sleep room.

Reuben could hear the tykes in the next room chattering at a whisper. He could pick out Kade's young voice in particular. Olivia was good about keeping their world at peace with a kind reminder that they needed to keep their voices down.

It didn't go unnoticed how Addy, Hunter, and Bang had stared Reuben down when he arrived. Not one asked the question on their minds. They were worried about their parents. Olivia kept them distracted—or, more likely, they kept her appeased with their willingness to play along with the charade of distraction. These children were far ahead of Clarisse, he suspected.

His last thought as he fell into some semblance of sleep was his daughter Lawoaka and how, at this moment, she and her mother were protecting him while he tried to recharge so he could cover them at night. *This can't go on. Not like this.*

"I'm going to run it!" Dutch yelled. "It's the only way to hold them back!"

"No!" Dalton hollered. "It's too late for that. They're gaining on us!"

A new explosion rocked the ground. Dalton collapsed out in the open. Shots pinged the ground before him, and he began to crawl toward cover by the Jeep. They had to push them away.

Then his worst nightmare came true. Seven jihadists sprung out of the woods and got the jump on Dutch. He lost his weapon in the melee and tried to fight them off by hand. One of the assailants held a Taser and piled on top of him while he screamed in agony. They finally pistol whipped him and drug him into unconsciousness.

~ ~ ~

"Nooo!" Dalton screamed. He woke by the dim lantern light in a full sweat. He remembered now, and twisted his head first one way and then the other as terror ripped through him. His entire body was on fire. He didn't know where he was, and for a second he thought perhaps he'd been captured too. He lifted his arms and realized he wasn't bound, just in a lot of pain.

On his right lay a form on a similar cot; to his left, another. He stared up at the ceiling and realized the corrugated metal meant only one thing: they were in one of the cache bunkers.

He lifted his head and looked around further. McCann had fallen asleep against the wall, near the entrance of their metal shelter, with his rifle across his lap.

"Hey! What the hell's going on?" Dalton asked. "McCann?" he called out.

"He's asleep," Sam said next to him.

241

"Sam?"

"Yeah, it's me."

"What the hell is going on?"

Sam emitted a long breath, and the delay scared Dalton.

"I don't know where to start," Sam admitted.

"Tell me this. Are my boys okay?" Dalton thought he'd start there and work his way down.

"Yes. I believe the kids got away and they're fine."

Dalton now remembered seeing Clarisse, and how pissed off at her he was. He swallowed before he could ask about her; his throat clenched at the thought. He remembered running toward a Jeep, but nothing else. "Is Clarisse . . . where is Clarisse?"

"She made it, Dalton, but she went back with Graham for Dutch. I couldn't stop her. I'm sorry." Sam's voice cracked with grief.

The sound of hope came from McCann. "They're coming back," he said in the darkness. "I know they will."

As Graham and Clarisse trekked through the forest, everything seemed like a dream. They smelled something like a barbeque the closer they came to the clearing at the cliffs. That and a foreign chanting filled the air. As they came closer still, their first vision into the camp was smoke wisping up from the ruins of the prepper camp and what was left of one of McCann's horses, brutally butchered when it couldn't escape.

"Get down," Graham said, and they lowered themselves behind the tip of a rock face. They inched forward on their bellies until they could see farther into the clearing of the former camp. If they were to fire from their position on the jihadists below, they would certainly attract attention and give away their location, but it would take a while for the enemy to climb the rock face to reach them. The cliff would also protect them from gunfire as long as they stayed low enough. Like all things, however, it was only a matter of time before they'd be discovered, so they had to devise a way to save Dutch and do it quickly enough to escape with their own lives.

"What are they doing?" Graham asked in a whisper. Several of the jihadists were chanting; others were on their knees, bowing.

Clarisse laughed. "Praying. They're such good moral citizens, remember?" She shook her head in disgust while she unloaded their ammo. "I had Muslim friends who died by their hands, too. They've killed off an entire planet in religion's name."

"I'm pretty sure this has Lucifer's name written all over it, if you ask me. Not that I'm a religious man," Graham said. Clarisse nodded in agreement while he set up the rifle on a stand so that he could aim, pivot, and hold the sight steady.

He scanned the area below. "Do you see Dutch anywhere?"

Clarisse looked at the charred remains of the prepper camp below, but he was nowhere in sight. "No. They've historically performed beheadings at sunrise. It's doesn't look like his body is anywhere on display, which is how they've done it in the past, so I'd say we made it in time for the festivities. He's got to be in one of those trucks or back in the woods, out of view," she said. "How are we going to get to him?"

"They are all pretty spread apart. We could . . . " Graham was interrupted by loud shouting began from below. "Damn," he said, hurrying to line up the scene through the scope.

"Oh, Jesus," Clarisse said as they dragged Dutch's bare, beaten body into the clearing. The jihadists formed a semicircle around him. The wild excitement they displayed sickened Graham. He'd seen this too many times on Internet video. He knew what would happen next. Everyone knew what would happen next.

"We . . . we can use the RPG and start firing on them. Maybe one of us could get to him in time," Clarisse said quickly.

"No, we'd only kill him in the process and—look at them, there are at least fifty of them. They'd get to us before we could wait until Dutch was out of the way."

Two of the assailants brought Dutch through the crowd, his arms tied behind him in a noose knot. They shoved him to his knees, without his prosthetic leg, in front of the ravenous crowd shrieking in delight of the festivities to come, shooting their guns into the air and wailing into the wind.

Graham's heart began pounding out of his chest.

Another man showed up holding a knife.

"Goddammit!" Graham muttered. Clarisse grabbed his shirtsleeve as he eyed the horrific scene below through the scope.

Clarisse pulled on him. "Graham! Graham! End this now. Kill him! Kill Dutch now! Don't let them have the pleasure!"

He knew she was right. He hated the thought of killing Dutch himself but knew he had little choice. It was the only way to save him. He'd hesitated before, once, when all of this had begun, and that hesitation nearly cost him and the twins their lives. It was a lesson he'd learned: kill or die. But this was different; this was kill or let die by the worst means.

He sighted Dutch through the scope as the killer stood before him, intoning his evil spell. The demon grabbed Dutch by the forehead and raised a knife, singing in a language Graham could not understand—nor would he want to in a million years. The assassin began to swing the knife toward Dutch's throat. The chanting heightened.

"Now! Do it now!" Clarisse begged again.

Graham aimed for Dutch's head. Dutch's eyes stared forward, and then looked up to Graham's position . . . as if he knew. Just as the blade began a crimson line, Graham shifted the sight a hair north and fired a single shot.

Knowing he would die, Dutch would want to go down with a fight.

Blood spewed backward in slow motion. Not only did the bullet end the assassin's life in an instant, but the chanting ended in abrupt silence. Dutch took advantage, and without the noose tension on his tied hands he scrambled forward, yanking the killer's knife from his dead hand. Another man looked up at their hidden position and yelled, "Allahu Akbar!"

As several jihadists surged toward Dutch, Graham began picking them off one by one. He watched as Dutch lunged and gutted one who approached him. Blood splattered over the ground. Dutch grabbed the man's discarded weapon, and with a knife in one hand and a rifle in the other, he shoved himself up off the ground onto his one leg. Dutch held his arms out in welcome for the next attacker as Graham continued to shoot at anyone who came near him.

Clarisse already had a round loaded into the RPG and fired from her shoulder as Graham began picking off the scattering crowd. She aimed and fired again after reloading. Pandemonium broke out below, and Clarisse fired on them repeatedly. Trees caught fire and, again, she rained hell on them, tears streaming down her face.

As Dutch massacred as many as he could, one lucky shot from a jihadist ended his life. In slow motion, Graham watched as Dutch was struck from behind and hit the ground.

He heard Clarisse screaming. It seemed far away.

A bloodbath lay before them, though several still ran for cover. Bullets careened off the rock face where they hid, sending chunks of it flying. "Time to go," Graham said, and grabbed Clarisse by the arm. They fled through the forest as fast as they could back to the waiting Jeep. Gunfire exploded chunks off a tree right in front of Graham as they ran. He pulled Clarisse behind him and took cover.

They both took peek shots around the cover and took out three more of the enemy before they chanced running for the next tree cover. Graham fired again as more movement through the brush headed their way.

"Get to the Jeep!" he yelled, shoving Clarisse forward. She ran as he covered her, and dove into the passenger side. Graham ran for it after taking out the last shooter.

They raced away. Graham heard nothing now; only his eyes recorded anything. He watched behind them through the flying debris, kicked up by the high speed of the Jeep, for any signs of a chase and glanced back at Clarisse. She wept openly as she drove, continuously wiping her tears on her sleeve to clear her sight as they put more distance between them and the remaining enemy.

It replayed in Graham's mind: The recognition on Dutch's face. The surprised silence. Seizing his chance to fight them. Dutch died fighting them. He died a hero.

I gave him a chance. He would have wanted to go down fighting.

"They should be back by now," Dalton said, his rough voice intoned with worry as McCann checked his blood pressure again.

McCann looked at him with near panicked eyes. "They'll be here, Dalton. I know Graham won't fail."

"Listen!" Sam yelled at them. The sound of a racing engine came in their direction.

"Open the door!" yelled Dalton. Sam grabbed his rifle and pulled himself over to the edge of the door, getting ready to fire at any oncoming enemy.

McCann tossed Dalton his rifle as he grabbed his own pistol. Rick still lay unconscious on his cot, unaware of the events taking place.

Dalton watched as Sam peered around the slightly open door. "It's them. They're back. It's our Jeep, and they're coming in fast," Sam said.

"Someone following them?" Dalton asked.

"I don't think so. Maybe Dutch needs care?" Sam speculated.

Clarisse stopped the Jeep and ran toward the doorway, like a deer fleeing danger. McCann opened the door all the way, and Clarisse ran into Dalton's one-armed embrace. He caught her, having thought he might never see her again. She trembled, and Dalton tightened his grip around her. "What is it? What happened? Are you hurt?" he asked.

"No, she's not hurt," Graham answered from the door. "Pack up. We've gotta go. Now!" Graham ordered.

"Dutch?" Dalton asked, holding Clarisse as close as he was able to.

Graham shook his head. "No. He's dead."

"Damn," Sam said.

Dalton stroked Clarisse's back, now knowing why she couldn't speak, and tried to comfort her after all the hell he suspected she'd just witnessed.

"Let's go!" Graham reminded them as he and McCann lifted Rick up and into the Jeep. "I'm sure they're following us."

Sam covered their every move until everything was loaded. They took as many supplies as they could but left much of it where it remained—locked up for another time, another day, when they might return.

"We'll be back," Dalton assured them all.

Graham drove toward the coordinates Dalton supplied from the passenger's seat. Clarisse sat with Sam and McCann in the backseat, and Rick lay in the cargo area, where she could keep an eye on him.

After a while, Dalton reached over the seat for Clarisse's hand. She still shook like a fragile leaf in a torrent, and he only imagined what she'd seen. In time the horrific events would come out, and he would be there for her when they did.

"Where are we going?" Graham asked as the miles flew on.

"North, to gather the others," Dalton answered.

"Then where?" Graham asked as he stared ahead to the open road leading away.

Dalton looked out his window as they sped off Highway 20, past the blurring trees that lined the Skagit River, and then turned left to hit the forest service road 1060. Cold, gray, desolate mountains loomed in front of them. Dalton hated to leave it, he hated to let the enemy have it. He vowed to himself that he and the others would return; their absence would be short, only long enough to make them whole. Then they'd be back.

They pulled past a section of road that looked much like the rest of the scenery they'd traveled past in the past hour.

"It's here somewhere," Dalton said, leaning upward to scan the woods closely for a sign of the entrance.

Graham slowed to a crawl. "Are you sure?"

"Yeah, according to Reuben's map, anyway," Dalton said. Graham stopped, and Dalton opened the door cautiously, only to hear a distinct click.

Mark appeared behind a wall of evergreen shrubs and smiled at him. "You made it, cousin! We were beginning to worry."

"Yeah, most of us made it," Dalton said. Mark waved to Graham in the driver's seat. When the smile left Mark's face, Dalton could tell Mark knew they were missing one.

Mark began to move the loose evergreen camouflage away enough for them to drive through. Dalton returned to the Jeep, and as Graham drove along the long, forested pathway, they went from day to dusk, a more fitting shade to match their somber mood.

He pulled up to a long, gray hunting lodge clearly bereft of care in recent years. Tala, with Sheriff by her side, appeared in the doorway with a smile, but it was Lucy that Dalton was concerned about.

They exited the Jeep, and amid the greetings, Dalton told them of the one they'd said good-bye to. He looked for the girl with the flaming red hair. "Mark, where's Lucy?"

"You passed her on your way in. She's down there. I think she knows already," Mark said.

Dalton peered back the way they had come, and then Clarisse touched his arm. "I'll find her. I should tell her," she said.

"Okay," he conceded He watched Clarisse walk up the drive toward Lucy's concealed position with Sheriff and one of Dutch's dogs trotting beside her.

"You made it!" Reuben said, interrupting Dalton's stare and shaking his hand.

"Yeah, just barely," Dalton said, heading inside the cabin with the others.

~ ~ ~

After the new arrivals had eaten, several of the adults gathered around a rustic harvest table that had clearly seen better days. They sat on various overturned buckets, tree stumps, and other things scavenged from the area.

Dalton called the meeting to order, even though he could still hear Lucy's muffled sobs in the nearby room. Clarisse said she took the news as well as possible, and that she'd be fine in time.

"Well, we're not safe here. We're not far enough away," Reuben said.

Dalton heard him out and agreed. This hunting lodge would never do in the long term.

Then Rick, who lay on a nearby cot, spoke up. "I say we split up. The guys will stay here and form a plan to fight them. The rest go farther north."

Dalton shook his head. "I'd like nothing more, Rick, but we're not ready. I'm not, and there's no way you're in any condition to fight them. No. That won't work right now."

"Where are we going to go, then?" Graham asked.

Dalton spread out a map on the uneven table surface, ran his finger from their approximate location to just north, and tapped his finger on a spot. "Here. It's the only town in reach, actually. There will be more resources for us to get ourselves together, heal, and formulate some kind of plan."

Graham looked down at the town.

"Where is it?" Tala asked from her position across the large table.

"Hope. We're headed north to Hope, British Columbia," Graham said.

Dalton scanned the solemn faces around the table and tried to reassure them. "We'll be back before long. And when we return, we'll be ready," Dalton vowed.

To be among the first to learn about new releases, announcements, and special projects, please follow this link or contact author A. R. Shaw.

Please consider writing a review for *The Last Infidels* on Amazon. Even a quick word about your experience can be helpful to prospective readers. Click here to write a review .

A. R. Shaw's titles include:
Graham's Resolution Series
The China Pandemic
The Cascade Preppers
The Last Infidels
The Malefic Nation

Kindle Worlds commissioned novellas
Deception on Durham Road
(Steven Konkoly's Perseid Collapse Series)
Kate's Redemption
(Blake Crouch's Wayward Pines Series)

A. R. Shaw, born in south Texas, served in the US Air Force Reserve from 1987 through 1991 as a communications radio operator, where she was stationed at the Military Auxiliary Radio System (MARS) Station at Kelly Air Force Base, Texas.

Her first novel, *The China Pandemic* (2013), climbed to number 1 in the dystopian and postapocalyptic (SHTF) genres in May 2014 and was hailed as "eerily plausible" and with characters that are "amazingly detailed." Shaw continues to write the Graham's Resolution series.

Shaw lives with her family in eastern Washington State where, after the deep snow of winter finally gives way to the glorious rays of summer, she treks northeast to spend her days writing alongside the beautiful Skagit River.

You can contact A. R. Shaw directly at AR@AuthorARShaw.com or through her website at AuthorARShaw.com.

No work of fiction is completed wholly on one's own. Research on any given subject can take weeks and even months and, more crucially, the help of several key individuals whom the author bugs on many occasions. Here I'd like to thank those who put up with my many questions or contributed in some way to this book.

Keri Knutson, Cover artist

Brian Bendlin, Editor extraordinaire

Beta Readers, you know who you are. Thank you, thank you, thank you!

Christopher Barber, veteran of the US Army, former paratrooper, and my cousin. Through your eyes I've seen the desert.

Christopher Armstrong, a Sam of sorts, my brother-in-law, and one who knows mantraps, the woods, and critter care.

Will Moore, police officer, competitive shooter, soon-to-be writer, and friend. Your weapons and officer training have come in handy!

Gil Gruson, HAM friend and sounding board. The radio knowledge I struggle against, even though it's a part of my past and my present; thanks for making it clearer to me.

Steven Bird, pilot, author of the Homefront series, friend, and inventor of the reapers. You are a plethora of knowledge.

W. J. Lundy, writer of the Whiskey Tango Foxtrot series. You had the answers to an essential question. Thank you!

My friends and Graham fans, because I was stumped for a title.

Oakley, Constant companion and my insight into Sheriff

My family, bringers of tea and snacks. You put up with my odd schedule and random questions, and work around my imaginary world. I love you guys!

CPSIA information can be obtained at www.ICGtesting.com
Printed in the USA
LVOW07s2259060116

469486LV00021B/1523/P